A famous playwright is dispatched in a most peculiar manner and left center stage in Carmel's beautiful Forest Theater. Riordan and Reiko, through careful sleuthing and a lot of dumb luck, manage to discover the identity of the murderer while resolving another, wholly unrelated situation. At no time during the course of this narrative does anybody suggest that Jessica Fletcher is the world's foremost mystery writer.

D0179341

**Playing God . . .
and other games**

Other books by Roy Gilligan:

Chinese Restaurants Never Serve Breakfast
Live Oaks Also Die
Poets Never Kill
Happiness Is Often Deadly

Roy Gilligan

Playing God...
and other games

Brendan Books
CARMEL, CALIFORNIA

Art direction by Robin Gilligan
Cover art by Reed Farrington
Photography by Splash Studios
Book design and typography by Jim Cook/Santa
Barbara

Copyright ©1993 by Roy Gilligan
Published by
    Brendan Books
    Post Office Box 221143
    Carmel, California 93922-1143
All rights reserved. This book, or any portion thereof,
may not be reproduced by any means without written
permission of the publisher.

Manufactured in the United States of America.
1–93

Library of Congress Catalog Card Number: 92-74052
ISBN 0-9626136-4-9

This one is exclusively for Jane, who for years has suffered the slings and arrows of outrageous fortune and miraculously survived being married to the author for a very long time.

AUTHOR'S NOTE

Now you know very well that if anything like the events in this book really happened, they'd have been headlined in the *National Enquirer*. So please accept the fact that this is a work of fiction and none of these things occurred, save in the fuzzy brain of the author.

My thanks and undying love go out to Robin, who created the cover design, and to Reed Farrington, whose abstract painting on the cover really sets the stage. My thanks to Will Smith, retired editor, for going over the manuscript and pointing out that I spelled "theater" in the Continental manner ("theatre") about seven hundred times.

Playing God...
and other games

1
Playwrights like playing God, I think.

I DON'T KNOW why it is, but weird things seem to happen to me during the summer tourist months on the Monterey Peninsula. Maybe it's because the tourists bring with them a carnival atmosphere, along with their tank tops and ugly shorts. Maybe it's because I am always in awe of people who can go around in beach costume when the temperature is in the fifties, the breeze is stiff out of the west, and the fog blots out the sun for long, long days.

I'm not really sure about that "carnival atmosphere," unless the word "carnival" is used in its seediest interpretation: a sort of traveling show, surrounded by game stalls where you can win the dolly for the little lady with an investment of only twenty or thirty dollars' worth of rings or baseballs.

It was an unusually bright morning early in July when Reiko marched into the office and announced:

"I am going to take you to the Obon Festival. It's time you learned a little something."

"About what?"

"About Japanese culture, dammit."

"I will not eat raw fish, Reiko."

"You do not have to eat raw fish, Riordan, although it's one of the best things you can eat for your health. Everybody knows that."

"*I* don't know that. Fish can be full of . . . *flukes* . . . or something. Like pork, you know. You've got to cook it a long time to get rid of the little things in it that cause trichinosis. It can. . . ."

"Forget the raw fish!" She was just a little exasperated. "You like flowers? You like teriyaki? You like tempura? I *will* meet you here Saturday at noon. You will accompany me to the Obon Festival at the Fairgrounds." She sat down hard on her Scandinavian knee stool, so hard that I thought she might bruise her tight little behind, and fell to manipulating the keyboard of her computer, a device that seems to grow new tentacles even as I watch it.

Reiko and I constitute an investigative firm on Alvarado Street in Monterey. The sign in the window now reads Riordan and Masuda as the result of a hasty promise I made a while back. Well, maybe it was about time. The little lady had been with me for more than ten years, and had been my good right (and sometimes left) arm during all that time. I love her like a . . . I'm really not sure. Daughter? Guess that should be the relationship: a lovely, oriental doll daughter. But I'm ashamed of the feelings I get sometimes. Sister? Na-a-ah. Certainly it's more than just friendship. Certainly not an "employer-employee" thing. I'll probably never sort out my true feelings for Reiko. She came into my life when I needed her most, and for that I'll be forever grateful. But that's a long story.

But as I said just now, things seem to happen during the summer months. And some of them are pretty dreadful. I wasn't thinking about that when I gave up the struggle and went into my office to do some heavy-duty thinking about a case an insurance company had me working on. It was one of those personal injury things that investigators get altogether too frequently. The deal is to try to determine if the alleged injured party is faking it. The insurance company would like him to be faking it so they don't have to put out any money. Insurance companies don't like to put out any money. And there are some attorneys around who aren't too terribly scrupulous about those things. I had a notion that this guy was really hurting, but the insurance people were paying me, so I had to try all the tricks. Unfortunately this often involves surveillance, and surveillance is a godawful bore. But, what the hell, there's the rent to pay.

The phone bleated—I can't say the phone rang any more. It's these new cheapie phones they're putting out. Reiko grabbed it quickly because the sound annoys her as much as it does me.

"It's Sally, Riordan." Then, in a sort of Japanese guttural, "Your main squeeze."

I hoped the hold button was down for that one. Reiko is not too crazy about Sally Morse, who has been my occasional roommate for the past few years.

"Sally, my love, what is it that I can do for, to, or with you?" I was jovial as hell.

"I don't know why I am attracted to you, Patrick. You are disgustingly vulgar in a naïve sort of way. I called to tell you of a small triumph of mine. I have at long last been cast in a speaking part in a play to be given at the Forest Theater."

"Aha, I have it! The part of the wife in *Sleuth*, a great one for you."

"Dammit, Riordan, you know as well as I do that the wife never appears in *Sleuth*. This is a new play by a famous playwright who prefers to remain anonymous for the moment. It seems that this is a new sort of thing for him . . . or her. It's semi-experimental."

"Is there any sex on stage? That would seem to me to be semi-experimental. I hear it's all the thing in New York these days. There was even a production of Hamlet where Claudius. . . ."

"Stop! I read about that. I know what Claudius did. It's *incredible*. Desecrating Shakespeare!"

"OK. Congratulations. You're an actress. When is this thing going to hit the boards?" I am conversant with show biz slang.

"We start rehearsal Saturday afternoon. The play is scheduled to open in mid-August. You're going to come and bring all your friends. That should not be a great financial burden."

I ignored the slight. "Fine. Are we still on for Saturday night?"

"I count the hours. Bye."

So twice in the space of only a few minutes I had been coerced by women. I had to spend Saturday afternoon listening to Reiko on Japanese culture, and Saturday evening listening to Sally chatter about how being an actress is so much more exciting than being a travel agent. Especially in a play in which the author chooses to remain nameless. Playwrights like playing God, I think. Maybe that's the only kick most of them get. Getting a play produced is about a thousand-to-one shot. Having it hang on and make money? As Papa Hemingway used to say, "Nada, nada, nada."

So I was in for a boring Saturday, unless something dreadful happened.

Fortunately, it did.

2

As I said, something dreadful happened.

PROBABLY YOU'LL have a struggle with this, but Saturday morning they found Benjy Noble's body lying in the middle of the Forest Theater stage with the long blade of a Swiss Army knife imbedded in his throat up to the hilt. To add to the theatricality of the scene, all of the knife's accessories were pulled out in different directions, and the toothpick lodged between Benjy's principal incisors. Benjy, who, I learned, was perceived (perhaps wrongly) to be an amiable fellow by *almost* everybody, had been badly beaten about the head and shoulders with a blunt instrument apparently before the knife was used. But I'm getting ahead of the story.

I didn't hear about the murder until much later. Iron-willed Reiko was determined to drag me to the Obon Festival. I didn't have the guts not to show up.

The Festival, I learned, is an annual event commemorating a Buddhist legend about a follower of the Buddha whose mother, a selfish old crone, was condemned to the hell of starvation. In that terrifying Buddhist place of detention, every time you try to eat, the food bursts into flames. When the disciple, Moggaliana, asked the Buddha for help, he was told to invite the villagers and monks to a feast of atonement. This got mama out of the hell of starvation into maybe a one-bedroom condo, causing the son to dance for joy with his buddies. So food and dancing have a lot to do with the Obon Festival.

For any event at the Monterey County Fairgrounds, parking is a problem. The town has tried to swallow the area, and there's no free parking lot. Reiko, who insisted upon driving, had called on her ancestors—or maybe just her multitude of relatives—to open up a spot right in front of the gate.

A small, cheerful elderly lady sat just inside the door alongside a box labeled "donations." Responding to Reiko's elbow in my ribs, I thrust a handful of bills into the slot and the lady handed us programs and a beautiful long-stemmed rose which Reiko tore from my hand, leaving red streaks across my palm. To our right several people were unloading a mountain of roses and carnations and the fragrance was delightful.

Equally delightful was the aroma of teriyaki floating in through a door in the back of the hall. I cheered up a bit as Reiko dragged me in the direction of that wonderful smell, but she had my wrist clamped in a vice-like grip as we passed the booth where the strips of marinated beef were cooking over glowing charcoal, and headed me toward another building.

Now I am not insensitive to the beauty of Japanese flower arrangements, nor am I unappreciative of the art of bonsai, but a whole goddam room full of the stuff gets to be a little much. After about a minute and a half my interest began to fade. People were oohing and aahing all around me, but all I could think of was the smell of the teriyaki beef that had followed us into the building.

My small companion, it appears, was obligated to examine every exhibit for an excessive period of time. She would observe from a distance of perhaps three paces, then slowly move in until her nose was touching the flowers or the bonsai. I've seen people do that in art galleries, but most of them are faking it. A lot of the people who haunt art galleries like to put on this little act, even when they're alone.

At last she was finished. She looked up at me with her blinding smile and said, "Let's eat." I sighed loudly and my stomach made a gurgling noise that could be heard throughout the hall.

My knees were a little weak as I pulled Reiko toward the teriyaki booth. She stood by impatiently, tapping her foot. When the girl in the booth had piled four skewers of fragrant beef on my plate, Reiko bolted into the main building and bought a plate of sushi, a bowl of noodles and a Kirin beer, setting an indoor record for the event, I'm sure.

When we sat at a long table featuring small flower arrangements all marked "$2.00," I complained mildly, "I've got nothing to drink. You know I don't drink beer or sake, and God knows teriyaki *doesn't* go better with Coke." Reiko waved one hand in the air while stuffing sushi in her mouth with the other. A smiling man in a hapi coat appeared with a pot of tea, poured me some in a styrofoam cup, and silently moved away.

While we ate, a voice with the slight Japanese inflections that occur even in the Nisei was exhorting the crowd to eat up and be sure to buy flowers. Then there was a pause, a squawk, and another voice with a heavier accent came on. I'm not going to attempt to render this as it sounded. There was the usual trouble with l's and r's. There's a lady at my bank in special accounts who has such a struggle with the pronunciation of English sounds that I cannot understand her at all. I just nod and smile and hope she isn't telling me my account is several hundred dollars overdrawn.

"Please attention," the new voice said. "Telephone Miss Reiko Masuda, please. Phone at bar, please."

She didn't miss a beat with her noodles. She twirled up the last on her chopsticks, tilted up the bowl and drained it, wiped her fingers and stood up, all in the same motion. She was off in the direction of the bar before I could turn my head and follow her.

In a moment she was back. "It was Sally, Riordan. She didn't know where you were, but she thought she might find me here. She's pretty shook up. The author of the play she's in, whatever it is. He was found dead this morning on the stage at the Forest Theater. She's at her office. Finish your beef and I'll take you there."

As I said, something dreadful happened. Fortunately. Otherwise, I wouldn't be telling you this story.

3
"Benjy Noble won the Pulitzer Prize last year."

SALLY'S OFFICE is upstairs in the Doud Arcade on Ocean Avenue in Carmel, over the hill from Monterey. But the Peninsula is really pretty small and Reiko is a driver of considerable skill and daring. We were there in under twenty minutes.

Reiko parked the car illegally, as is her wont, around the corner on San Carlos, and I dashed through the side door of the arcade past the fragrance of Paolina's Italian restaurant, which for the first time lost its usual allure for me, and up the stairs to Sally.

Her door was locked. Through the glass I could see her sitting at her desk, staring at a wall poster advertising the wonders of Singapore. I banged on the door a couple of times. She seemed not to hear, so I hit the glass with my big university class ring. The sharper sound and the possibility of the glass breaking seemed to shake her out of her trance. She rose slowly and opened the door. Her face was gray and her eyes glazed.

"We got there about noon, Pat. There were police all over

17

the place. There was an outline of the body in chalk right in the middle of the stage. Did you know they really *do* that? Draw a chalk line around a dead body. Inside the head part of the drawing there was a lot of blood. They'll never get that stain out, Pat. They'll have to paint the stage. Or stain it. Or put new boards in or something."

Sally moved around the room as she spoke, her arms folded across her chest, her hands gripping her shoulders. Her chin was down so that her voice was muffled. She didn't appear to look where she was going, but she didn't bump into any of the furniture.

I could imagine the scene at the Forest Theater. It's outdoors, as the name implies, surrounded by a stand of tall trees, a beautiful setting. The seats are just bare benches arranged in a semi-circle and they can get pretty hard during a long show. But the regulars know what to do: bring a cushion to sit on, bring a jacket against the chilly nights (even in midsummer, *especially* in midsummer), and get a seat near one of the fireplaces if it's really cold. There's a great stone fireplace at each front corner of the rows of benches. One of the important jobs of the staff is to keep it stoked during the plays.

And I could just see the Carmel Police on the scene. God, they must have been excited. A bizarre murder right in town. Sure as hell beats traffic arrests, fights in bars, vagrants sleeping at the Mission, or barking dogs. Lots more fun than chasing kids on skateboards, or warning surfers to keep the sound down on the stereo.

I live in Carmel in a quaint one-bedroom cottage owned by a gentleman I call George Spelvin, although that isn't his real name. I don't talk about all the work I have done for George, and he doesn't charge me any rent. It's a damn' fine arrangement. The only disadvantage of the deal is that George keeps a lot of stuff in the garage and I have to park my car outside. This isn't so bad. Lots of cars are parked outside in the village of Carmel-by-the-Sea. But that's the problem: the sea eventually gets to 'em. Like what has happened to my beloved Mercedes 450 SL, bought with the insurance money after my one and only wife was killed in an accident on Highway 280 near San Francisco. It was a beautiful car, but several years of salt air have got to it. That and a couple of mild fender-benders at unmarked intersections in Carmel.

It was because of the car that I had my first contact with the Carmel police. During the earliest months of my residence, I conscientiously draped my little two-seater with an expensive custom car cover every night. One night somebody came along and stole it. Next morning, when I had discovered the theft, I phoned the police to make a report.

Within minutes a patrol car was at my door. A serious young officer took an elaborate report and examined the car, the driveway, the garage (padlocked), and peered up and down Sixth Avenue. He walked over Santa Rita street to Ocean, looking for God knows what. Tread marks? Foot prints? He called me four times in the next two days to report that nothing had been found. I think it was the most exciting case he had handled since he had joined the force. Of course, that was long before the visit of the Pope a few years ago.

Sally was still pacing, silently. I grasped her gently by the shoulders and sat her down in her desk chair. "Want me to take you home, honey?"

She looked up at me. "Pat, there's no reason in the world why I should be so upset about this thing. I didn't really know the guy. I met him at the reading. He was introduced to us jokingly as "Anna Leiser," the name he wanted attached to this play. Get it? Analyzer?"

"I'm really pretty swift, honey. It's not the worst pun I've ever heard. But I've never heard of Benjy Noble, either. What did he write?"

Sally became more her usual self. "My God, Riordan, you are an ignorant dolt when it comes to the arts. Benjy Noble won the Pulitzer Prize last year. The Critics Circle Award. The Tony for best play. For *Memories of Jackson*."

I tried not to let on that none of what she told me rang a bell. "Oh, yeah," I said, brightly.

"You're trying to shine me on, pal. You don't know what I'm talking about. You have no feeling for art."

"Wait just a goddam minute. You know I paint. I've been painting for a lot more years than I've known you."

"You paint pictures of dogs, Riordan. I have that little black Lhasa on my wall. It's cute. But it sure as hell isn't art."

Sally was normal now. The light had returned to her eyes. She swiveled around toward me, hiked her skirt up to mid-thigh, opened the bottom drawer of her desk and put her feet on it. "You know Harold Denby?"

"By reputation. One of the important people in the Forest Theater group. Lives next door to where Paul Anka used to live, up on Jacks Peak. Next door is about a mile and a half."

"He's an old friend. He knows about you. Probably from George Spelvin. He wants you to investigate Benjy Noble's murder."

4
"Get him, Riordan."

THERE WAS NO real reason for me to get involved in a murder case. I told Denby that when I called him. But he had another notion.

"It's not as if it were the first time, Riordan. George tells me you've been very successful at homicide investigations."

"Lucky. Lucky is the word. I have not solved a single goddam murder case. Things seem to fall in my lap. Sherlock Holmes I'm not. Please let me refer you to John Miller of the Carmel Police."

"I know Miller. He's a fine cop. But I don't think he's particularly . . . intuitive. I'm willing to pay you, Riordan. For a private mission, if you will. Benjy Noble was an old friend and a major talent. I want to know why somebody killed him in such a bizarre fashion. The police are pretty good at ordinary crime. Murder for money, murder for passion, those they can understand. But . . . do you know how they found Benjy? It was awful."

"Something about a Swiss Army knife stuck in his throat with all the accessories out. Even the little scissors. I've never had one with the scissors. But, then, I've never had a bicycle or an electric train." I immediately wished I hadn't made that crack. There was a stony silence on the other end. After a long pause, Denby spoke:

"Maybe you're *not* the man for the job. Maybe George was smashed when I called him. Maybe. . . ."

I was contrite: "I'm sorry, Mr. Denby. I say things like that now and then. It's not that I don't appreciate the seriousness of this matter or your concern for Noble. Maybe I just like to take the pressure off with flip remarks. For my own sake, sometimes. For George . . . and for Sally . . . I'll take a crack at this case. Can't make any guarantee. And I've got other bread-and-butter work going now. I won't charge you unless I do you some good. How's that?"

At the other end, Denby was thinking about it. You can't hear a man scratch his head or stroke his chin on the telephone, but I could imagine it. I had never really met the guy. I'd seen him at some of the larger soirees (I never get invited to the small ones), and God knows I'd seen his picture in the Pine Cone social pages often enough.

Finally: "Let's try it, Riordan. But I insist on paying you. I pay my way. Come to my office tomorrow at ten. I want to talk to you face to face. I have some knowledge that might help your investigation. You know where my office is?"

"Carmel Rancho Boulevard. I looked it up before I called you. See you at ten tomorrow."

Carmel Rancho Boulevard is the rather pretentious name for what is essentially one long block between Rio Road and Carmel Valley Road. There are some pretty nice new office buildings on it that have gone up in the last decade. I had found Denby's office address listed under his home address in the phone book, but I had no idea what kind of business the guy did. As far as I was concerned, Harold Denby existed only in the misty world of George Spelvin and friends—people who played lots of golf and went to lots of parties and drove Bentleys. They were not truly of my world.

After my phone chat with Denby, I leaned back in my

swivel chair and put my feet up on the desk. This position enables me either to think more clearly or to fall asleep, whichever happens first. That day, I thought. For a while . . . until I dozed.

Reiko woke me up. "Post time, Riordan. Ed Braverman from West Coast Fidelity Insurance awaits you in the outer office."

There *is* no outer office. Reiko and I are separated by a thin partition, half glass and half wood panel, with a door in the middle. Even with my window open on Alvarado Street I can hear her pop her gum in the "outer office."

"Show the bastard in," I growled, affecting the demeanor of the seedy, shifty private eye.

"You are some kind of crazy, Patrick," said Braverman, coming through the door. "I don't know how you stay in business. Well, maybe I do. It's that sterling little partner of yours here, a lady of charm and intelligence. How'd she get stuck with you?"

I've known Ed for a long time. We both worked out of offices in San Francisco until we both got smart and moved to Monterey. San Francisco was an exciting and beguiling place when I got out of the Army in '54. I guess any place would have had a lot of charm for me after foot-soldiering in Korea. The old town stayed pretty charming until the late sixties or early seventies when the changes began to be overwhelming. Too many goddam tall buildings, too many people, too much yuppishness. Too many saloons. But there had always been too many saloons. After my wife was killed, I got thrown out of most of 'em.

The Monterey Peninsula has been growing pretty fast, though. I'm not sure how long the charm will last here. But maybe I won't live long enough to see tall buildings on Alvarado Street or yuppie condos on Cannery Row. That's a comfort.

"I have not caught your boy in any shenanigans, Ed. I've checked him by night and by day and he's never been out of the wheelchair. I've even sunk so low as to peek in his bedroom window. His wife has to help the poor bastard go to the bathroom. I think he's legit."

"Try some more. We have some background on this guy. Either he's the unluckiest man in the world or the most creative. He's been involved in two other accident cases in other states. We exchange information with other companies, you know. He got big settlements both times. Give it at least one more shot, Pat."

"It's your money. You are paying me by the day, plus expenses. This guy might eat in some very expensive restaurants."

"I'd rather pay your expenses, however exorbitant, than kick in a hundred grand to a faker. Get him, Riordan."

How I was going to "get" the guy, I had no idea. But the money was good.

"OK. I'll have Reiko make a pass at him. If that doesn't get him out of the chair, nothing will." A muffled squeal came from beyond the partition. She's always tuned in.

Ed and I exchanged perfunctory leave-taking remarks with the usual insincere mentions of getting together for lunch. I decided to do something about the Benjy Noble murder. The urge to nap had left me.

The place to start would be the Carmel Police. I rang their business number and asked for Lieutenant Miller.

"Miller. Can I help you?"

"Pat Riordan, John. Will you be there a while? I want to talk to you about the DB at the Forest Theater. A philanthropist is paying me to check on it."

"Come on up, pal. There sure isn't much to go on. Somebody really gave the little fruit a going over."

"Are you implying that Benjy Noble was gay?"

"Aren't all those theater guys? I thought that went with the territory."

"You mean you don't really have any knowledge of the man's, uh, sexual preference."

"Well, no. But it's something to consider, don't you think. Gay-bashing is a common form of amusement with some folks."

"Don't jump to conclusions, John. What do you know for sure?"

"Honest Abe confessed to the murder. Said he did it because Noble had stolen his play. We fingerprinted him and let him go. He liked that."

Abraham Andrew Atterbury, also known as "Honest Abe" in these parts, is a local eccentric who lives in a van which is parked in Carmel until the Carmel police chase him, or in the county until the Sheriff's men get after him. He routinely confesses to every major crime on the Peninsula.

"Is that it, John?"

"Yeah. Except that we have an eyewitness who saw somebody come out of the Forest Theater at three in the morning . . ."

"Hang in there. I'll be right over."

5
Alison Hargrove's house was easy to find.

As I DROVE over to Carmel, it dawned on me that having an eyewitness to something that occurred in the vicinity of the Forest Theater at three in the morning would be the highest form of serendipity. The town is very dark at night. There are no streetlights, and after sundown the stranger who ventures off Ocean Avenue on foot had better have a powerful flashlight. On foggy nights it is deeply black. You literally cannot see your hand in front of your face. So whoever it was who saw somebody leaving the scene of the crime in the middle of the night must have remarkable vision or an overactive imagination.

Miller was in his office when I arrived. It wasn't exactly his office; there were four or five desks in the room, and the Lieutenant's was one of them.

"I really ought to have walls, Riordan. Like the news guy on 'WKRP.' But I haven't got the guts to put masking tape on the floor to show where the walls should be. Sit down."

I pulled up a small chair and sat. Miller's desk was stacked with reports and other important-looking papers. To the front was a small sign that read, THANK YOU FOR NOT SMOKING. In a corner was a five-by-seven photograph tilted just enough toward me that I could see a red-headed kid and a woman's arm.

"All right, John, what's this about an eyewitness?"

He drew a long, deep breath. "This woman lives up behind the theater. I mean you got to be a lover of the stage to live up there. You can hear every sound in her living room. Can you imagine what it must be like during one of those bagpipe concerts?"

"Well, go on with it."

"OK. She went to bed after the show that was on Friday night. What was it? I dunno."

"*Our Town.* Wilder. Go ahead, *please.*"

"Anyhow, she went to bed. Along about two thirty in the A.M. she woke up. Claims she heard a sound she couldn't identify. Her story is, she lives alone, and can ID any noise she hears any time of day or night. So she heard this noise. She goes out on her deck. Between her deck and the theater there is a fairly big cypress just behind the lighting control booth but she can see through it when the stage lights are on. She thought she heard the sound again, so she dashed back into her house and got this humongous flashlight—must carry eight batteries—and shone it down on the stage. She didn't see Noble's body. But she did catch a glimpse of a figure dashing down the pathway to the parking lot. I asked her if she heard a car. She said no, the guy must have been on foot."

He looked at me, expecting some sort of comment.

"That's it? That's your eyewitness?" I was just a tad angry. Or maybe I was really angry. "I could have had you give me that over the phone."

"I get lonely, Pat. Nothing but cops up here all the time."

I shook off my anger quickly. Miller is a thoroughly likable guy and an excellent policeman. He had told me all he knew up to this point about the murder of Benjy Noble, and I was sure he'd tell me when he knew any more.

"Got a name for the flashlight lady, John?"

He picked up a scrap of paper from his desk. "Here it is. Alison Hargrove. No middle name. House is on Guadalupe, right above the theater, big gray house. You can't miss it."

"I take it this is an older woman we're talking about?"

"She wouldn't give me her date of birth. She's somewhere between sixty and a hundred."

"Eyesight?"

"She wears glasses. But so do I, Patrick. Well, contact lenses."

"Honest to God, do you think she can really give us any help?"

Miller leaned back in his chair. "One thing I learned long ago is never to discount information just because there's some doubt about the source. So maybe she couldn't see much. But her hearing is apparently very damn good. She couldn't immediately describe the sound she heard that got her attention. All she could say was that it was a foreign sound, a sound she wasn't used to. Maybe it'll come to her, what the sound was. Maybe it'll help. Maybe not. Go on up and talk to her. Maybe she'll remember something else."

I drove to my house at Sixth and Santa Rita, parked the car, and walked over across Ocean and up a block to Guadalupe. The traffic on Ocean was bumper to bumper going down into Carmel. Some folks never learn that there are other ways of going down into the quaint village made justly famous by the election of Clint Eastwood as mayor. No matter how many times they may come to visit, they take the Ocean Avenue turn-off down the hill. On a sunny day in July, the line never ends. Some of the residents along Ocean never get out of their driveways on those days.

I didn't have far to walk. Living as close as I do, I go to all the shows at the Forest Theater in the summertime. They've done some pretty good ones. There's a lot of talent around the Peninsula, not all of it amateur. There are some retired pros and some young performers who are of professional quality. Monterey County sustains a raft of excellent theater companies. There's a new one a-borning, run by a friend of mine who writes mystery novels. Not much of a job for a man, but he seems to make money at it. And the actors do it mostly for love, like they say in *A Chorus Line.*

Guadalupe runs crookedly downhill on the east side of the theater. Alison Hargrove's house was easy to find. I walked up the flagstone path and rapped on the door with a rusty knocker provided for the purpose. And waited. I heard a faint stirring inside. I waited. More stirring. Waited. Rapped very lightly again. Waited.

At last the door opened a crack.

"Yes?" The word was pronounced carefully, extending the vowel sound in a rising inflection. The voice was husky and musical.

"Is it Miss Hargrove or Mrs. Hargrove?"

"It is *miss,* sir. Who are you?"

"Miss Hargrove, my name is Patrick Riordan. I'm conducting a private investigation into the murder of Benjy Noble. Lieutenant Miller of the Carmel Police said you saw somebody leaving the Forest Theater near the time of the murder. I'd like to have a little chat, if it's all right."

Alison Hargrove opened the door with an exaggerated flourish. She flung it wide, and nodded for me to come in. The entry hall was dim. She led me into a warmly decorated living room flooded with the sun from a skylight. She motioned me to a couch situated before a huge stone fireplace. Miss Hargrove took a position on the slightly raised hearthstone and looked at me expectantly.

She was a smallish woman with a halo of curly white hair around a face that showed signs of plastic surgery. The skin was taut over the cheekbones, and the corners of the eyes seemed to be under tension. The nose had come under the knife at one time, probably long ago. There was the unmistakable extra space between the eyes that give a nose job away every time. Alison had been a striking woman in her younger days, but now the cosmetic surgery was betraying her. She had tried to compensate with too much make-up; he eyes looked out of sockets that were too dark, her brows were penciled in too perfect an arch. Her mouth was red, really red. I thought of Gloria Swanson in *Sunset Boulevard*. She stood there, silent, waiting for me to start the conversation.

"It must be quite, ah, interesting to live so close to the theater that you can hear everything that goes on." A lame beginning, but I couldn't think of anything else.

She tilted her head back and stroked her hair with a thin, delicate hand. From the diaphragm came a wonderful musical laugh. She opened her eyes wide (like Gloria Swanson), and said:

"I glory in it, Mr. Riordan. The theater . . . is my life."

6

"I saw what I saw as well as you could."

As if cued by the lady's announcement, the shaft of bright sunshine from the skylight shifted just enough to catch the halo of white hair, and I fully expected some sort of demonstration of the occult. But the feeling passed in an instant. This was a person of the theater, a woman of indeterminate, if advanced, age, a small person whose once fine features had been pulled and stretched in an effort to forestall the inevitable marks of time. She had struck a heroic pose before me, and was waiting for me to speak.

"So you were an actress, Miss Hargrove," I said, lamely. "What productions might I have seen you in? Did you do any films?"

She stepped down from the hearth with great dignity and arranged herself in a chair covered with flowered chintz to my left. It was obvious that she wanted me to have the full advantage of her right profile.

"I worked on the Broadway stage for more than thirty years, Mr. Riordan. In many productions that never reached the West Coast. It seems a pity, although probably they would

have been misunderstood in California. As for motion pictures," her face took on a shade of subtle superiority, "I did
appear in a few, unfortunately in subordinate roles. There was
a time when I needed the money. That was before I met Mr.
Halvorsen, my late husband."

"Oh. When you told me it was *Miss* Hargrove, I assumed
that you hadn't been married. It's sort of what you assume
when a lady. . . ." I was floundering a bit.

"In the *theater,* Mr. Riordan, one does not abandon the
name with which one has won fame. Mr. Halvorsen under-
stood. I have always been Alison Hargrove, *never* anything
else."

I had almost forgotten what I came here for. The woman
was the closest thing to a witness to the murder of Benjy
Noble. At least, she *heard* something.

"Miss Hargrove, you told Lieutenant Miller that you were
disturbed by an unfamiliar sound which roused you from
sleep on the night of the murder. Can you remember anything
about that sound?"

She closed her eyes and touched her forehead with the fingertips of her right hand.

"The Lieutenant asked a similar question. I have tried.
Even now I am trying to recreate in my mind the events of
that night. I woke up. I heard the sound. I seized my flashlight
and walked out to the deck. There was another sound, like
footsteps on the path. I pointed the flashlight down into the
theater. A figure was running down the path to the parking
lot. I just got a quick glimpse of it."

"Could you tell if it was a man or a woman?"

"It was a brief impression. It could have been either."

"Were you wearing your glasses, Miss Hargrove?"

She bristled a bit. "The Lieutenant told you I wear glasses.
I had asked him as a gentleman not to mention that."

"Did you wear your glasses?"

"Yes I did, sir. I keep them on my bedside table. They cor-
rect my vision to twenty-twenty. I saw what I saw as well as
you could."

"If you hadn't worn your glasses, what could you have seen?"

"That is an impertinent question. I need not wear the glasses . . . except in certain situations. Mr. Riordan, my first impression was that you were a reasonably attractive person with definite, if minimal, charm. I'm beginning to change my mind."

"No offense, ma'am. I just have to ask questions to get as much information as I can in a situation where there isn't much information. And to this moment, you're the only person with any information." I heard myself saying these things unconvincingly. "About the noise. Have you had any second or third thoughts about that?"

The eyes closed and the hand went again to the forehead. "I know that the sound was one with which I was unfamiliar. I have lived in this house for eight years. I can identify bird calls, skateboards and leaky mufflers. I can even eavesdrop on conversations in the audience down there during intermissions. I can determine the speed of the wind by the sound. There's a young man who plays the piano very badly in a house a hundred yards away, and a young couple next door whose bedsprings make a sound that annoys me almost every single night. I don't know how they can keep up the pace. But the sound that woke me at something after two on Saturday morning was not one of those. At this moment, I cannot call it up in my memory."

I decided it was time to go. "Thank you, Miss Hargrove. I'd appreciate it if you'd give me a call if you can remember more about the sound. Or if you hear it again. Better call Lieutenant Miller first. Then me. Here's my card."

She studied it carefully. "You have a partner, Mr. Riordan. A Japanese partner. It is hard to believe that we were once at war with those people, isn't it. This Mr. Masuda. Is he perhaps a modern day Samurai?"

"Yes, he certainly is," I said without hesitation.

The lady showed me to the door with slow and measured steps. She shook my hand gravely and assured me that she

would call if she remembered anything more about the night
of the murder.

When I got to the street, it dawned on me that I was very
close to the scene of the crime, so I turned down the hill on
Guadalupe towards the Forest Theater. It's a steep descent
down the hill to Mountain View, and around the corner to the
theater parking lot. Nobody was in sight when I entered into
the theater grounds. Nothing seemed out of the ordinary. The
usual yellow tape used by police to keep people away from a
crime scene was gone. It had been on just long enough to can-
cel the Saturday and Sunday performances of *Our Town*.

I climbed up on the bare stage. There was a set that suggested the outline of a small town upstage, but nothing else.
In most performances of *Our Town* a character called Stage
Manager improvises the props as the play goes along. I hadn't
seen this production, but I guessed it wasn't any different.

The chalked outline of Benjy Noble's body was still there,
smudged but visible. Somebody had tried to scrub out the
bloodstain without much success. Sally was right. They'd
have to do something to mask that stain.

I looked up at Alison Hargrove's house. I could just make
out the deck through a gap in a big cypress tree just behind
the shack that is used by the lighting people at the plays.

There is something of the ham in me, always has been. I
was in all the plays in college, a prominent member of the
Drama Club. And here I was in the middle of a stage, with a
golden opportunity.

I imagined an excited, expectant audience out front, which
was here just to see me.

Seizing the day, I made a deep bow to my imaginary public. Then, hunching my back with one shoulder in the air, I
limped downstage and began: "Now is the winter of our dis-
content made glorious summer by this sun of York. . . ."

"Riordan, what the hell are you doing?"

I turned to see Sally Morse and four or five people I didn't
know standing upstage. Two of them began a burst of vigor-
ous applause.

7

"You're a marvelous character for a play, Mr. Riordan."

T HE ONLY appropriate gesture I could think of was a deep and courtly bow. I pretended to remove what might have been a plumed hat and swept my arms backward in a contortion that I must have seen in a dozen Shakespeare plays. Or it might have been in an Errol Flynn movie.

"I thank you, in the King's name, my friends."

"Riordan, you're a nut," said Sally, obviously embarrassed just to have to acknowledge before her friends that she knew me. "These people are members of the cast of Benjy Noble's last play. We've come here to rehearse."

I looked them over with my experienced investigator's eye. A tall skinny youth of perhaps twenty-five with a bad complexion. A middle-aged matron with badly dyed red hair. A pretty ingénue with protruding breasts. A steely-eyed, gray-haired man of fifty or so with a clipped mustache. And a woman dressed all in black with severe black eyebrows and jet black hair pulled into a ponytail.

"Don't let me interfere. I'm just here because of a little old murder. I realize the show must go on."

Sally sighed and reluctantly began to introduce me to her associates. "This is Sean Wetherby," she said, indicating the pimpled youth. The matronly red-head was introduced as Cordelia Pompilio. "She was named after the character in *Lear*, you know." The ingénue was Christy Burgess. She smiled winningly and squeezed my hand.

The fiftyish fellow was introduced as Templeton Hedges. He nodded curtly. "And this is our director, Maria Theresa O'Higgins. She's directed nearly all of Benjy's plays."

The woman in black advanced and embraced me, planting a wet kiss on my cheek. "You are Sally's very special friend. I can tell. Is he good in bed, Sally? I might borrow him sometime."

Sally blushed. I think it was the first time in many years that she had blushed. But she turned a bright pink, and lost her usual icy control for just a few moments. "He's a dog painter, Maria. No real stamina. Hal Denby has seen fit to hire this turkey to investigate Benjy's murder."

Maria Theresa flashed black eyes at me. "Ah, you are showing the police how it should be done."

"No, ma'am, I'm just poking around, helping the police if I can. Can't get in their way, you know."

"So modest," said the director. "You're a marvelous character for a play, Mr. Riordan. Something by Mamet. Or Neil Simon."

"Funny, I had always fancied myself as a character out of Eugene O'Neill. Shows you how wrong a guy can be. But don't let me hold up the rehearsal." I smiled at each of them, climbed up to fourth row center and spread myself out in the sunlight.

For the next two hours, until the sun began to hide behind the trees to the west, I tried to understand what was going on on the stage. The title of the play, I gathered, was *Waiting for the L Train*, which suggested to me Odets' *Waiting for Lefty* or Becket's *Waiting for Godot*. Me, I was waiting for Sally.

She was watching me out of the corners of her eyes at all times while struggling through the dialogue which to me was unintelligible.

From what I could get, the play was set in a New York subway station. The characters all had set places and poses on the stage, and each took turns with short monologues. What the audience is supposed to get, it seems, is an insight into the lives of five lonely people in New York who never really know each other, although they leave for work every day from the same subway station.

After the first hour, following a long harangue by the gray-haired gent with the mustache, I felt my eyelids growing heavy, and for the second hour had to consciously tell myself to stay awake. So this was experimental theater. I would much rather have seen Claudius do what he did to Gertrude in that avant garde production of *Hamlet*. Or see the little ingenue with the big boobs in *Oh, Calcutta*.

At long last, Maria Theresa raised a black-sleeved arm in the air and snapped her fingers. This was the signal that the rehearsal was over. Everybody looked relieved and left the stage. Except for the older of the males, who remained center stage, mouthing soundless words.

Sally made her way up to me with a mildly threatening look on her face. "Why did you do this to me?" she asked.

"I didn't do anything to you, Sal. I just happened to be here when you guys arrived."

"You didn't have to stay. I was embarrassed to death to have you out there watching me. This is a hard play to get into, and I don't need any kibitzers."

"What's the play about? I just watched it for two hours and I'm damned if I know."

"This was a *rehearsal*, dummy. Wait until you see the performance. Then you'll understand it."

"Do *you* understand it?"

"Well . . . no."

"Oh."

Sally was sitting on the bench beside me. I hooked my arm

around her neck and kissed her. She seemed to loosen up then, and moved closer to me. "This whole thing is near to being a disaster," she said. "At first, everybody just thought we'd call the production off. But Denby and the others insisted that since we were privileged to premiere the play, and had already paid a pretty good fee to Noble, we'd carry on. It seems spooky to me. I cannot understand the play, and neither can any of the others in the cast, except Temp Hedges, but I've always thought he was full of bullshit. Maria Theresa may be a great Broadway director, but she's no help at all to us. I don't know what I'm saying or what it means most of the time. Oh hell, Riordan, why couldn't I be Nellie Forbush in *South Pacific?*"

"Because your hair would fall out if you washed it that often," I said, comfortingly. "Let's go have a bite and then out to your place for some horizontal aerobics."

Which we did.

8
"Loss of services, he says."

SALLY LIVES about eight miles out into Carmel Valley, where it's a lot warmer in the summer and colder in the winter. I have entreated and cajoled, but I can't get her to come in and live with me. "It's too damned cold in the summer," she says. "I like warm sunshine. I have to *work* in Carmel during the summer, and some days I freeze my ass. Why don't you come out here?"

It does no good to tell her I can't stand the heat in the summer, and I'm getting to an age when I have trouble with the cold in the winter. I do what I can to ignore the aches and pains, and pretend that I'm thirty-nine. But nobody's fooled.

When I stay over at Sally's I have to take my own car. I'm an early riser and she's a sleep-in. So on that rehearsal day, I had to go back to the house and get my own wheels. So, with first light the next morning I was able to get up, dress, make a pot of coffee and shake Sally goodbye.

She acknowledged a kiss on the forehead with a faint moan, and rolled over. I tiptoed out.

I stopped at the Wagon Wheel on the way into town for a

big ranch-type breakfast. I don't often get the chance for a hearty repast in the morning. Most of the time I make do with a cup of coffee and a piece of toast, unless I wait until I get to the office and bully Reiko into going to the bakery down the street for pastries. It's all stuff I shouldn't eat: the pastries are full of coconut oil, and the Wagon Wheel's breakfasts are orgies of cholesterol. But, what the hell, I say. You got to go from something. My Irish grandfather ate hog jowl every day of his life, and chewed uncured tobacco he grew himself. He was in his eighties when he died, and he never heard of cholesterol or the dangers of nicotine.

Feeling stuffed and a little ashamed, I drove back to the house for a shower and a shave. If I leave shaving equipment at Sally's, she uses it on her underarms and dulls the blades.

After cleaning myself up, I lay down on the bed for a while.

Maybe Sally's not kidding. Maybe I do lack the old stamina. But, as the fellow said, I may not be as good as I once was, but once I'm as good as I ever was.

At nine, I called my office.

"Riordan and Masuda. How may we help you?" Reiko sounds so goddam cheerful in the morning.

"Hello, honey. I've got a date with Harold Denby in Carmel at ten, so I'll be in late. Maybe about eleven-thirty, depending on what he wants to talk about."

"I tried to get you all yesterday afternoon. Ed Braverman has been trying to reach you. Some new development in the Talbott case."

"What do you mean, new development?"

"He didn't tell me. He never takes me into his confidence. He still figures you're the numero uno of this organization." She sounded miffed, and, I guess, rightfully so. I'll have to speak to Braverman about that.

"Did he leave a number?"

She gave me the insurance man's office number and hung up.

Talbott was the guy I was watching for Ed's company. I

had almost forgotten about him for the last few days, so engrossed had I become in Benjy Noble's murder.

When I got Braverman on the phone, he dropped a little bomb on me. "Talbott's lawyer called me yesterday. The guy's wife ran out on him. Now they're asking for a million bucks. That'll get the wife back, the lawyer says. Loss of services, he says. That's what made her leave."

"Loss of services," for the uninitiated, means, in legal language, that a guy can't get it up anymore. So, this injury to Talbott not only got him in the wheelchair, but it also deprived him of his manhood, or the standing symbol thereof. If the injury is legit and not feigned.

"So what do you want me to do? Recommend a urologist?"

"This may be just another clever ploy, Pat. This attorney doesn't seem to be very bright, but you never can tell. Can you intensify the surveillance?"

"Sure, I'll get right on it. Don't worry. Leave it to me." These were meaningless sentences. I had no idea what I was going to do about Talbott. I called Reiko again.

"Look, pal, I am going to be tied up with this murder thing, at least today. Can you do a little snooping at Talbott's house for me?"

"What do you want me to do? Make a pass at him, like you told Ed Braverman?"

"From what I hear now, honey, I'm not sure that would do any good. But watch the house. Just sit in the car and watch the house for a while today. You never can tell. And I owe it to Braverman."

"If you say so. Just tell him I can be trusted with the facts." She can sound real snippy when she wants to.

By this time, it was getting close to quarter to ten, so I figured I'd better get going to Denby's office. I suspected he was one of those guys who set great store by promptness, and I didn't want to be late. I found out later that I was dead right.

Harold Denby Enterprises had a suite high up in a building on Carmel Rancho Boulevard. This area, at the mouth of

Carmel Valley, has grown briskly in the last ten years. For a while it was just a couple of grocery stores and a huge parking lot. Now there are three clusters of shops, the old rancho group by Brinton's Hardware, The Barnyard, and The Crossroads. The latter two are trendy and high fashion, with a couple of good restaurants. The more recent developments include a just-finished bank building and a post office. The offices have been around for a while and the rate of occupancy seems to be pretty high now.

Denby's receptionist, a prim, business-like woman in her thirties, stood to receive me and asked me to have a chair until she could announce me to Mr. Denby, who was on the phone. Would I like a cup of coffee? No, thank you, ma'am.

In a few minutes I saw her mutter a few words into her phone, cupping her hands around the receiver. She looked up at me and smiled, "You may go in, Mr. Riordan."

I touched my forelock and bowed stiffly. Her smile froze a bit and she nodded nervously at the great man's door.

Denby was standing behind his desk when I entered, and he came forward to meet me halfway across the quarter-mile of deep carpet between the desk and the door. His handshake was cordial and practiced, and my big university ring bit into my fingers as he clamped down on my hand. I hid my wince as best I could.

"I'm not sure our association will last long, Mr. Riordan. Since I talked to you yesterday, information has reached me that may pretty well clear up the mystery of Benjy Noble's murder."

9

"Sincerely yours, Paul Lindemann."

DENBY INDICATED a chair for me. It was a terribly uncomfortable chair, and I suspect that the idea was to get rid of callers as soon as possible. I began to get the notion that Harold Denby was a master games player, and the realization made me uneasy. After a silent interval, he spoke:

"Benjy had been staying at my house on Jacks Peak. We were old friends. I met him years ago in New York when he was a struggling unknown. I had the opportunity to invest in one or two of his early plays. Both of them lost money for me, but in my tax bracket . . . well, let's just say it did no real harm. I regret that I was not in contact with him when he began to have his successes. After our early acquaintance, we were out of touch for quite a while. A year ago last spring, when I had to be in New York on business, I went to his Pulitzer Prize play, *Memories of Jackson.* It's a marvelous piece of work."

Denby had assumed a pose that I've seen in portraits of successful businessmen, head forward, both palms planted on desk, eyes boring into me, the victim.

I cleared my throat. "Just for my own information, Mr. Denby, what is your business."

"My business is *businesses*. I buy and sell them. I am a self-made man, Mr. Riordan. Unlike many of the people who live at my level, but have inherited great wealth. I began in the banking business as a teller forty years ago. Now I have more than enough money. There's no need for me to continue in business. But it has been my life."

"At my level." I didn't much like the sound of that. Too much like a voice from Olympus. But I deal with people at that "level" all the time. Most of them are the type that Denby was not, like George Spelvin. Good old George exists for wine, women, and an occasional song.

Denby had paused, obviously pleased with himself. "To continue. Benjy had been staying with me. He was excited about his new play, *Waiting for the L Train*. He told me he believed it was the best thing he had ever written. Suggested in all innocence that it might be worth a second Pulitzer . . . or another Tony. That was nonsense, of course. Those things are all so political. Benjy would probably never win another award of any kind."

"O'Neill and Robert Sherwood both won three Pulitzers," I said, "and it seems to me that Stephen Sondheim's won at least a couple of Tonys. So . . ."

Denby cut me off. "I suspect that I am not as familiar with theater lore as you are, Mr. Riordan." He glanced at his watch. "But we must move on. As I was saying, Benjy was staying at my house. After his death, I felt it incumbent upon me to go through his personal effects. Perhaps I was not within the letter of the law in taking this action, but it is now done. In a briefcase I discovered some correspondence that might bring us to a conclusion on the case."

"Did you tell the police about this correspondence?"

"Well, no. But I plan to turn the briefcase over to Lieutenant Miller. I see no need to inform him that I'm aware of its contents. But in the name of discretion, perhaps you could take a few steps before the police can turn the bureaucracy loose."

At first I thought that Denby just simply had no respect for our local authorities. But then a vague suspicion began to gnaw on me. Why all this sneaky stuff? Why did Denby hire me in the first place? Did he have something he wanted hidden? I filed these dislocated thoughts in the back of my mind, where I keep "theater lore" and old restaurant menus.

"So, what about the correspondence?"

He drew a packet of letters out of his top desk drawer and handed them over to me. "Read them for yourself. I plan, of course, to return them to the place where I found them. But for the moment, where the official world is concerned, they don't exist. Take them into the outer office. I am expecting an important call from Amsterdam at any moment." He dismissed me with a wave of his hand.

In the outer office, after fending off another cup of coffee from the painfully efficient receptionist, I found a comfortable chair in a corner and slipped a rubber band off the bundle Denby had given me.

The letters were addressed to Noble at his New York office. There was no return address. There were three envelopes, each fairly fat with its contents. I checked the postmark dates and opened the earliest one.

Page after page was full of single-space typing, apparently on an old manual machine that produced many broken letters. I began to read. The first two or three lines made little or no sense. I went back over them. They still wouldn't work for me.

Slowly I went through the densely typed pages and it finally came through to me that the writer was accusing Benjy Noble of plagiarizing a work of his, a play about a group of people in a subway station. I glanced back at the date of the letter. It was April 23 of the current year.

The second letter was more of the same, dated May 15. The third letter (June 10) was stronger, hysterical in tone, still barely intelligible, and signed, as were the others, "Sincerely yours, Paul Lindemann." Except in the last one, just before the "sincerely yours" there was a line that read, very clearly,

"If you do not publicly acknowledge my contribution to this play, I will find you and kill you."

Authors are pretty jealous of their work. And they're often unstable people who live in a world of the imagination. But they seldom threaten anybody. Most people who write are peaceful creatures . . . with the possible exception of Norman Mailer. There have been plenty of lawsuits involving who thought of what first and got it down on paper. Most of them fade away with little or no money changing hands. But it's a matter of pride, you know.

Who the hell was Paul Lindemann?

"The name doesn't mean a thing to me," said Denby, when I finally got back into his office. "That was what was so unusual. I should have thought that Benjy would have mentioned this matter to me. Or he might have reported it to the police in New York. But he did neither. Can you draw any conclusions from this? What is our best move?'

"Give this stuff to Miller. Have him check with New York. See if they've got anything on Lindemann. I don't know how important this stuff is. It's really pretty weird. It might mean a lot, or it might be just a lot of crap. But if it was important enough to Noble to keep it in his briefcase, he must have attached some significance to it."

I slipped the rubber band back over the envelopes and handed them to Denby. He took them gingerly between thumb and forefinger and dropped them into the drawer as if they were full of cholera germs.

"I'll replace them in the case, Mr. Riordan. And turn it over to the police. I trust this evidence will help bring this matter to a close."

"Maybe it'll help. But it isn't evidence. There's a long way to go before we can really figure out who killed Benjy Noble."

10
"They kicked me out. Nice people."

I GOT BACK to the office just before eleven-thirty. Standing in front of my door with a look of doom on his face was Templeton Hedges, a fellow cast member of Sally's. When last I had seen him, he was posing in the fading light on the stage of the Forest Theater, mouthing his lines silently to an absent audience.

"I had a hell of a time finding you," he said.

"You could have looked in the phone book."

The face went blank and the eyes crossed slightly. He hadn't thought of that. I dragged out my keys which are secured to a ring that features a brass simulated ticket to *A Chorus Line.*

"Well, is it?" he demanded.

"Is what?"

"The play! Is it going to be produced? Or is Denby calling it off? I've got to know. It's the best goddam part I've had with that crowd and I don't want to lose it. What's your connection, anyway?"

I remained calm. After all, what did I have to get excited

about? "I have no connection with the Forest Theater organization, Mr. Hedges. I have been retained to investigate the murder of Benjy Noble. I think Sally mentioned that yesterday. If that's all that's bothering you, set your mind at rest. I can't stop the play, and Harold Denby tells me he doesn't intend to stop the play. So go home and practice your lines."

My words were meant to relieve Hedges' mind, but judging from the expression on his face, they didn't have much effect.

"Is there something else, Mr. Hedges?"

He peered up and down the hall. "Is there some place where we could talk?"

"We are at the threshold of my office, Mr. Hedges. There is no reason in the world that we can't go in and sit down and make ourselves comfortable while you say what you have to say, whatever that may be." The man was obviously jittery, but somehow I found the situation funny.

He followed me into the office. Reiko, I assumed, was out checking up on Charles Talbott, the guy in the wheelchair that Ed Braverman wanted caught walking or standing or *in flagrante delicto* with anybody.

I walked around behind my desk expecting Hedges to sit down, but he didn't. I opened the window to get some air in the place, sank into my favorite piece of furniture, and put my feet up on the desk. Hedges stood tensely in the middle of the room.

"OK, if you're not going to sit down, say your piece. Or recite some lines from *Waiting for the L Train*. Don't just stand there."

He seemed to be trembling slightly. He put his hand on the back of my client's chair for a moment, then made what seemed to be a difficult decision to sit down in it.

He began in a semi-whisper, quite unlike the stentorian tones I had heard from the stage during the rehearsal. "Yesterday . . . at the theater . . . you met all of us. That is, Sally introduced us . . . and told us what you were doing there. Do you remember the other man in the play . . . Sean Wetherby?"

"I remember a string-bean kid with lots of pimples."

Hedges looked spooked. "Yes, I guess you could describe him that way. Well, during the first few readings, Wetherby kept trying to change his lines. Benjy would not hear of it. Sean kept whining about being made to say things he didn't understand. Benjy got really angry and threatened to replace Sean. They got into a shouting match. It was pretty funny to watch. Benjy Noble was about five-three and a little on the stout side. Sean must be six-four and skinny as a rail. All of a sudden, Benjy turned and walked away. Just walked out of the room. I heard Sean mutter some things to himself. I'm sure I heard the words 'kill the bastard'."

"Don't we all say things like that in a fit of pique, Mr. Hedges? Hardly incriminating."

Hedges persisted. "I know Sean. I've known him since he was in grade school. He's trouble. He always has been."

"Noble kept him in the cast, didn't he?"

"Yes, and Sean pretty much kept his mouth shut during later readings. But yesterday—when you were there—I guess nobody else noticed it but Sean was reading his lines as he had wanted them, not as Benjy had written them. And, of course, there wasn't anybody to stop him. Doesn't that throw suspicion on Wetherby?"

"I sure wouldn't convict on that. *But* . . . I'll have a little chat with Sean. Any idea where I can find him?"

"He lives alone, in a little furnished room in Carmel. It's in back of a house on Lobos. Used to be a garage, but a lot of them have been converted, some of them illegally, you know. Lobos, between Second and Third, I think. You might knock on a few doors and ask."

"You said you've known the kid since grade school. Does he have family here?"

"They kicked him out. Nice people. Neighbors of mine at the Point. He just got to be too much for them." Carmel Point is an area of pricey homes just to the south of Carmel proper, but not within the town limits. I've got some pretty well-to-do clients on the Point, but no Wetherbys.

"What did the kid do?"

"Drugs. From the time he was about fourteen. What really pissed off his old man was the time when Sean got coked up and creamed a flawless '67 Rolls convertible. Maybe it wouldn't have been so bad, but the Rolls belonged to a guy down the block and Sean destroyed his father's Continental in the process."

"What does the kid do to support himself?"

"He's a busboy at one of the Carmel restaurants. I don't know which one now. He moves around. Breaks a lot of dishes, I understand."

I leaned back and examined the anxious face of Templeton Hedges. He was exceptionally well-groomed and dressed. He had an expensive haircut, and wore a conservatively cut natural shoulder suit. "What do you do for a living, Mr. Hedges?"

"I'm a stockbroker. Partner in the firm of Callaghan, Benson & Reid. Offices in New York, San Francisco and Monterey."

"If you're a partner, why isn't your name on the door?"

He remained stone-faced. "The names are those of the founding partners. They're all dead. Maybe they'll add my name when I'm dead." He was serious.

I shepherded Hedges out of my office with a hand on his shoulder and reassured him that I would pursue indefatigably the miscreant or miscreants involved in perpetrating the crime. I pick up a lot of my language from police reports.

As he was going down the hall, Reiko came from the other direction.

"Got news for you," she called. She looked pretty confident. She sort of struts when she's very proud of herself. She grabbed me by the arm and dragged me into the office.

"I parked across from Talbott's house. A guy drove up and went in. A big guy. Pretty soon, out he came with Talbott in the wheelchair, put him in the car with the chair in the trunk, and drove off. I followed them at a respectable distance. So what happens? He pulls up in front of the Marriott downtown, just a couple of blocks from here, lifts Talbott out of the car and back onto the wheelchair and takes him into the hotel. I parked at the corner in a 24-minute zone and ran into the hotel. Got into the same elevator with the guy and Talbott. Followed them off as cool as you please. I hung back when they went into one of the rooms. The big guy came out alone and went down in the elevator. I waited a while and then knocked at the door. Nothing happened for a moment or two. Then the door opened and there's this woman in a negligee. I could see Talbott in the bed—it was a king-size bed, Riordan, the biggest goddam bed you ever saw —and then I excused myself and said, 'Wrong room, sorry,' and came back here just now."

She was out of breath and so was I. "And so what do you think it all means, Reiko-san?"

"Don't you see, Riordan? He was performing a service for the lady. A definitely incriminating act!"

11
"Are you obstructing justice, buddy?"

I DIDN'T HAVE THE heart to tell my elated partner that what she saw really wouldn't mean anything in court. Maybe the lady was a masseuse. Maybe she was involved in special therapy. Maybe Talbott was just tired. What the hell.

"Thank you, my dear. Just one thing. Did you by any chance get the identity of the lady in the negligee?"

"No. But I understand that there are services of that kind that can be summoned with a telephone call. Although I've never met anybody employed in that . . . industry."

"Tell you what, Reiko-san. See what you can do about finding out who the lady is. Surely one of your relatives works at the hotel."

"As a matter of fact my cousin Tak is on the desk there. Yeah, I'll check with him. But he doesn't come on 'til three. Right now I've got a lunch date. Greg's coming to pick me up. He's found a place in Seaside where they serve the best hash browns on the Peninsula."

Greg Farrell is an eccentric artist with an irresistible charm for Reiko and all the other members of her gender. Bearded, recklessly handsome, on the cusp of middle age, he lives down the Big Sur coast in a rustic cottage, unheated save for a single quartz appliance that he can carry around and plug into the precarious wiring of the place. I have warned Reiko repeatedly that he is a practicing rake, whose only interest is in her firm little body. Then he crosses me up by taking her to art shows, rodeos, and cartoon festivals at the Dream Theater. And he is also my good friend. But I have to project the fatherly image toward Reiko to sublimate my own occasional lust.

"The paint-stained wretch is going to appear again. How did you manage to get him out of his lair? Did you call him?"

She drew herself up proudly. "Of course not. Greg called me last night at home. We talked for an hour. He's making a special trip to get a plate of those hash browns. *And* he just thought I might like to tag along."

I had never known Farrell to spend more than fifteen or twenty seconds on the phone. He hates the device with a passion. "I only have it for emergencies," he says. When he makes one of his own infrequent calls, he leaves obscene messages on answering machines, which he also hates with a passion. And he loves his solitude so much that *his* phone is frequently unplugged.

"You and Greg got some kind of thing going?"

"Don't be silly. We're just friends. We have a lot in common."

It is hard for me to believe that this little partner of mine, raised in a strict Japanese family atmosphere, educated at a respectable university, always immaculate in appearance, should have anything in common with a shaggy painter from Big Sur who got himself blown up in Viet Nam. But I have just about given up trying to understand all the facets of Reiko Masuda.

At that moment, Farrell appeared in the door. "H'lo, Pat. Hi, babe."

"Babe! You let this throwback to the cave painters call you babe!"

I turned my face away in pretended disgust and fury.

"No offense, Pat," said Greg. "I asked permission. She likes it."

Reiko giggled. "I'm ready. Just where is this place we're going?"

Farrell was leaning over to kiss her on the cheek. "Out on Fremont in Seaside, near Broadway. Doesn't look like much, but the food is aces. Lot of guys from Fort Ord go there when they can."

"There is some Pepto Bismol in my bottom left desk drawer, Reiko-san. When you get back. And don't forget to get in touch with your cousin Tak, remember?"

She looked at me sharply. "Where are you going to be this afternoon?"

I hummed a couple of bars of *"Che gelida manina,"* and tried to look dreamy. "Oh, I don't know. Just here, I guess. With my thoughts. Nobody has asked *me* to lunch."

"Gee, Pat." Farrell looked genuinely concerned. "You could come with us if you want."

"Thanks, but no thanks. Ever since I had my gall bladder operation I've had to be pretty careful. But go ahead. Bless you, my children."

They went out the door hand in hand. A mild panic arose in my bosom. What if they should get married? Reiko's mama-san has always been suspicious of her attachment for me. God knows what she'd think of Greg Farrell. I'm sure it wouldn't bother him to convert to Buddhism. But he could never become Japanese.

I became aware of the sound of the phone, which might have bleated a couple of times while I was lost in my thoughts.

"John Miller, Pat. Harold Denby just delivered a briefcase belonging to Noble. There's a packet of letters in it. He kind of hinted that you knew something about it. Are you obstructing justice, buddy?"

"Denby showed me the letters, John. He's a kind of slippery type. I'm not sure I really trust him. I read 'em and told him to take them to you."

"Well, I've sent the guy's name to New York, but I figure it's a drop in the ocean unless he has a record. I'll let you know if anything comes through. There's one thing new that interests me, and it may be right down your alley. We got a call from a woman in San Jose this morning. She had read about Benjy's death and was pretty shook up. Apparently she had been out of town on some sort of seminar for several days and hadn't seen any papers. When I asked her what her interest was, she was pretty reluctant to say anything. But she identified herself as Dr. Pamela Hudson, and gave us her address and phone number. Want 'em?"

"Sure." I took down the information and thanked Miller. He scolded me mildly again for reading the letters before he could, and made it very clear that he would not protect me from the law if I didn't report anything else about the case to him immediately.

I pulled the San Jose classified phone directory out of a stack I keep on the floor in one corner of my office. I try to keep directories from all the major cities of California close at hand. Saves a lot of hassle with information. I flipped through the San Jose book to "Physicians." Running my finger down through the H's, I stopped at "Hudson Pamela M.D., practice limited to psychoanalysis." The address was a downtown building. Dr. Hudson was a shrink, by God.

San Jose and Monterey share the same area code, but you have to punch "1" before the prefix to make anything happen when calling from town to town. I tapped out the numbers idly, not expecting much.

To my surprise, the voice that answered at the other end said, "Dr. Hudson speaking."

"Oh, yeah, Doctor. My name is Patrick Riordan. I'm calling from Monterey. You see, I'm a private investigator working for an interested party in the matter of the death of Benjy Noble. I understand you knew him."

There was a long silence. Then the voice came on again: "Mr. Noble was a patient. Ordinarily, I would flatly refuse to divulge any information that results from the doctor-patient relationship. You must understand that. But in the case of a particularly ugly homicide. . . . One thing I know. I can't discuss the case on the telephone. Perhaps if you'd come to San Jose and identify yourself properly, I could be of some help."

"How about this afternoon?"

"Let me check my appointment book. Can you be here at three o'clock sharp. I have an open half-hour."

"You've got it, doctor. See you at three."

12
It was a place decorated to produce tranquility.

THE TRIP from Monterey to San Jose usually takes about an hour and fifteen minutes, or maybe an hour and a half, depending on whether you go through Castroville over to Highway 101, or up Highway One, through Santa Cruz and over the mountains on Highway 17. The mountain way is the quicker but more hazardous. Some folks I know flatly refuse to take that route. They think the percentages are against them, I guess. But I'm convinced it's six of one, half a dozen of the other. So on this occasion I chose the scenic route, up the coast to Santa Cruz and over the hills to Silicon Valley.

It was after one o'clock when I walked down Alvarado Street to my car, plucked the familiar parking citation off the windshield and took off for my rendezvous with Dr. Pamela Hudson.

I've made this trip so often over the years that the car pretty much knows where it's expected to go. Like the milkman's horse of long ago that pulled his wagon down the street

while he ran from doorstep to doorstep with his jingling bottles. Can I remember things like that? Very dimly. Maybe I
heard my father talk about it, maybe not. But there were still
horse-drawn vehicles in the days of the Great Depression.
Lots of people couldn't afford automobiles. I swear I can
remember the folks talking about when the Hindenburg blew
up. They were scared to death Hitler was going to come over
and drop bombs on us. He never did, but I think he sure
would have liked to.

These are the kinds of thoughts that flow through my head
when I drive. It's no wonder I miss off-ramps and landmarks.
But I wasn't going to miss the sign that indicated downtown
San Jose.

This town has sure changed over the years. Most of the
time when I come up to the Santa Clara Valley, I'm headed for
one of the electronics firms I work for from time to time.
Almost never get downtown. I've visited with Reiko's parents,
who live in the Willow Glen section. But I seldom have occasion to get down on First Street. When I arrived on that day's
mission, several new high-rise buildings surprised the hell out
of me. I checked the address of Dr. Hudson on a scrap of
paper I had taped to the dash of the Mercedes. I knew where
that building should be, but I was dismayed at the shiny glass
giant I found. I pulled into a parking garage behind the building and looked at my watch. It had been a longer trip than
usual. It was five minutes before three.

The directory in the lobby told me that the Doctor's office
was on the fourteenth floor. An elevator door was standing
open a few feet away. It began to close as I stepped inside and
just missed grabbing my left heel. I punched the proper button
and fought my claustrophobia for some long seconds until the
thing arrived at fourteen.

I found Dr. Hudson's office with no problem. Her name
was modestly lettered in gold on the door. When I tried the
handle, though, I discovered that the door was locked. I
tapped discreetly. In a moment the door was opened by
Pamela Hudson herself.

She was a tall woman, taller than I, and thin, with the figure of a model. She had those square, pointy shoulders from which hung a very fashionable dress of a silk print material. Her face was a model's face, with a thin, perfect nose, a full mouth, and a dimpled chin. Her eyes were a very pale blue, and her hair, which had apparently been carefully coiffed, was badly mussed, as if she had the habit of running her fingers through it.

"Mr. Riordan? Please come in. My assistant is off today having her teeth straightened. And I'm with a patient right now. Please wait here. It won't be long."

I had sat in Harold Denby's office that morning, and was sitting in Pamela Hudson's office in the afternoon. An office is an office. I sat on a leather couch and picked up a magazine from a glass coffee table. I flipped through the pages of a 1971 *National Geographic* and dreamed of my youth when I was electrified by those pictures of bare-breasted native women. But all I found in this issue was a full-color spread on a festival in Katmandu. I wondered idly if they still play polo with human heads in those places.

Abruptly, the door to the inner office opened and a frightened-looking young girl came out, dabbing her face with an already soaked handkerchief. "Thank you, doctor," she said. "I feel so much better." She burst into tears. She sure didn't look like she felt better. Dr. Hudson put an arm around the girl and led her out into the hall. I could hear a Pamela Hudson's low voice through the glass, but I couldn't understand what she was saying.

Eventually, the doctor came back into the office. She stood with her back to the door and sighed. She looked strangely vulnerable at that moment.

"Anything I can do?" I blurted.

She smiled. "Thank you, Mr. Riordan. I just feel so damned sorry for that little girl. She has such problems. And I'm not sure I'm helping her very much."

That admission cemented my impression of Pamela Hudson. Any doctor who would admit something like that to a perfect stranger must be a pretty decent person.

She pulled herself up to that formidable height and came over to me. At that moment I wished I was six-two, at least. I was almost afraid to stand up. I have nothing against tall women, you understand. But I feel just the least bit intimidated when they're taller than I am.

"Come into my office, Mr. Riordan. My next patient is due at three-thirty. Of course, the sonofabitch is always late, but. . . ." She looked embarrassed. "Did I say that? I must be more disturbed than I thought. Mitzi always does that to me."

We entered the inner office. It was a place decorated to produce tranquility. The colors were right, the light was right, the couch was right.

"How do you treat claustrophobia, Doctor?" I asked, thinking of my aversion to elevators.

"I really don't, Mr. Riordan. But there's a man in Palo Alto I could send you to. Unreasoning anxiety is the great bulk of his practice. He's the best in the country, I think."

"Never mind. I'm sorry to get off the beam like this. I'm here to talk about Benjy Noble."

"You'll forgive me if I ask for some identification. I have to be pretty careful."

I showed her my PI license, my drivers license, the ATM access card from my bank, my Macy's charge card, and my charter member card for the Monterey Bay Aquarium. She seemed satisfied.

"If you want anything else, please feel free to call Lieutenant John Miller of the Carmel Police. He may tell you I've got some outstanding parking tickets, but he'll vouch for my character."

She seemed more relaxed. "Benjy Noble was referred to me by a colleague in New York City who had been working with him for several years. I don't think you need the other doctor's name. I wouldn't give it to you anyhow. When Benjy came to me, I did a preliminary interview. Naturally, the doctor in New York had given me a run down on the case. Benjy had been undergoing treatment for a terrible depression. He appeared to be particularly depressed at our first meeting. And a little frightened.

"As our interview progressed, he became increasingly tense. When I pursued a series of questions designed to get at the root of his condition, he suddenly leaped from the chair you're sitting in and screamed, 'I killed him, I killed him!' Then he fell silent and wouldn't answer another question for the rest of that hour."

13
"Do you think he really killed somebody?"

P<small>AMELA</small> H<small>UDSON</small> looked pretty badly wrung out. The almost perfect model's face sagged a little, and the eyes were glassy.

"Are you sure you're in the right business, Doctor?" I said because I meant it. "There are some folks who can deal with the crazies and some who can't. How long have you been doing this stuff?"

She looked at me and smiled ruefully.

"I've been doing analysis for five years now. I've been under analysis for seven. But that's a professional must, you know. The analyst must be analyzed by another analyst. And that analyst must. . . ."

"I get it. A carrousel of neuroses. And nobody ever gets the brass ring. I'm sorry, Dr. Hudson, but it doesn't sound really scientific to me. Hell, I've got to read people every day in my business. And I'm right more often than I'm wrong. But back to business. What do you think Benjy Noble meant when he confessed to killing somebody? Who did he kill? Or had he imagined a murder?"

"I had only one more session with Mr. Noble. When he arrived, he seemed perfectly calm and cheerful. We exchanged meaningless observations about the weather. We had a comfortable hour, during which he talked freely about his early life, his failures, his remarkable successes, and his high hopes for his new play. He told me he was supervising the production being presented under a pseudonym in Carmel. He embraced me when he left, smiling and full of confidence. As he went out the door, he stopped and turned and told me he didn't expect to see me again." The lady had full control now and was the matter-of-fact medico I had expected to find in the first place.

"Do you think he really killed somebody?"

"I honestly don't know. Manic-depressives are hard to manage. And since all mental illnesses are more or less related, they can slip into paranoia on occasion. Benjy Noble was a brilliant playwright. I had seen one of his plays when a road company arrived in San Francisco. When I got the call from my New York colleague about Benjy's coming to the West Coast, I got his other works out of the library and read them all in one night. I am not a theater buff, Mr. Riordan, but I was able to visualize the plays of Benjy Noble just in the reading. Literature does not usually affect me that way."

A thought struck me. "Weren't you expecting somebody at three-thirty. By my watch it's almost four."

She smiled and sighed, as if relieved of a huge burden. "I told you the sonofabitch was always late. Looks like he's not coming at all today. This one is badly twisted, Mr. Riordan. He's a voyeur, an obscene caller, and a flasher. I'm doing him for the Municipal Court. He's a scrawny little man in his mid-fifties who always shows up looking like a wimp, with a little clipped mustache, bangs slicked down on his forehead. I know he's here when he gets off the elevator because he drenches himself in cheap cologne. Then he spends his entire hour telling me of his past conquests. At the end of his narrative—which I am able to interrupt only by speaking very loud—he invariably invites me out for a candlelight dinner, and looks pitiful when I refuse. I don't know whether I'm doing him any good or not, but he hasn't been picked up since I started seeing him. Maybe he gets off on confessing all those fictitious love affairs."

"Is there anybody else coming?" I asked.

"No. With Ellen—my assistant—out for the day, I usually run a shorter schedule. She's a big, healthy girl, Mr. Riordan, a runner and a swimmer. I feel safer when she's around. Some of my patients could really be dangerous."

"How about I buy you a drink someplace? Help you relax."

"That's the best thing anybody's said to me all day. There's a place just a couple of blocks from here that's quiet and soothing. Not full of yuppies lying to each other."

San Jose, unlike the Peninsula of Monterey, is hot in the summer. I hadn't noticed it so much when I arrived, although the air-conditioner in the Mercedes needs a charge of freon and doesn't refrigerate like it should. I had parked, walked maybe a hundred feet into an air conditioned building, still wearing the jacket I had on when I got John Miller's call. When Pamela Hudson and I walked out of the building shortly after four in the afternoon, it was like coming out of a casino in Las Vegas in August. The heat slammed me in the face, and the coat came off in seconds.

I again became conscious of the Doctor's tall figure as she walked beside me. I'm five-eleven and maybe a small fraction. Pamela Hudson was at least six feet plus heels. God knows it was six well-arranged feet, but I felt conspicuous walking at her side. I kept hoping she'd slump a little, but she had a model's carriage as well as the face and the body. I was relieved when we arrived at a small, dimly lit lounge, wonderfully cool and quiet, and she led me to a table in the corner. Sitting down, she didn't look so threatening.

She ordered a gin and tonic and I asked for one of those non-alcoholic beers that I customarily drink in situations like this. She looked at me curiously.

"You don't drink?"

"Nor smoke, nor chase girls. I try to be pure of body as well as mind and soul."

"What is it, Mr. Riordan? Are you a health nut?"

I told her briefly of my past, how my wife was killed, how I made an honest effort to consume all the Scotch whiskey in San Francisco until Reiko came along and took charge. "I don't know if I could get back to drinking moderately or not. But I think it's wise not to try."

She nodded in her professional mode. "Nobody knows right now. Although you are probably aware that there is a new theory out that insists that compulsive alcohol consumption is *not* a disease. Even though the medical profession has labeled it that way."

"No matter. The way I see it, booze makes you feel smart and talk dumb. It makes you embarrass yourself and forget about it. It makes you lose great chunks of your life. I can do without it very well. I can also do without the hangovers."

"You've almost convinced me," she said, taking a large gulp of her gin and tonic, "but not quite. This and maybe a little wine at dinner are all I ever use. And one of these is quite enough after the kind of day I usually have."

We sat for a while making small talk. Pamela Hudson told me she was originally from Pennsylvania, had graduated from Stanford in 1969 (rapid mental calculation told me she must be forty-twoish), and Harvard Medical School in '72. She had done her internship *and* residency at Massachusetts General, and came back to California to set up a private practice in San Francisco. When she found that San Francisco had almost as many psychiatrists as lawyers, she moved to San Jose which, at the time, was full of various types of mental illness resulting from the stress and strain brought on by the rags-to-riches, riches-back-to-rags nature of the electronics industry.

I was just in the middle of my own story, which involved my legal education after the Korean War, my loss of a fiancée just before my bar exam, and the world-class hangover that caused me to flunk it miserably. Just as I was about to tell her

why I never tried the bar again, a voice called out from across
the room.

"Pam. That you? Well, I'll be damned."

I turned my head to see the approaching figure of Harold
Denby.

14
"That sounds strange to me, somehow."

I HAD BEEN facing away from Denby, and when I turned around and he got a good look at me, the expression on his face was a picture. He had apparently smiled broadly when he discovered Dr. Hudson, and when he saw me, the smile sort of froze in a lop-sided way. He stopped short ten feet from us.

"Riordan. You are probably the last person I expected to see here. And in the company of Dr. Hudson."

She was puzzled. "So you two know each other. That doesn't seem too terribly strange. You're both from Monterey."

I spoke up. "We haven't known each other long, Doctor. Mr. Denby is the one who hired me to investigate Benjy's murder."

We looked at each other for a full minute before anybody said anything. Then Denby regained his composure and said: "Well, Riordan, you're better than I thought. You found out that Benjy was seeing Dr. Hudson. We tried to keep that pretty quiet. As far as I know, only Benjy and I knew of his visits to her office."

"Yeah, Mr. Denby. It was a brilliant piece of detective work. The Doctor called the Carmel police when she heard about the murder. John Miller called me. I called her. Sheer genius."

He settled in a chair at our table. "I'm in a way responsible for Pam's association with Noble. Charles Cartwright, Benjy's doctor in New York, is an old friend. So is Pamela. Charles called me when he learned that Benjy was coming to the Coast. Naturally, I referred him to Dr. Hudson."

"Well, that seems to explain things. Just a case of one old friend recommending another old friend. Then you must have been aware of Benjy's association with Cartwright."

"I told you that I had invested money in Benjy Noble's early plays—and lost. One of my co-investors was Charles Cartwright. He had known Benjy as a child. The families had lived on the same street in College Point. That's in Queens, you know. Charles was much older than Benjy. He had remained single and lived at home all during his professional training. He didn't marry until his mid-thirties. By the time Benjy was trying to get his first works produced, Charles was a successful psychiatrist in Manhattan. We met at an investor's run-through of the first play.

"Neither of us lost faith in Benjy Noble. We knew he had that spark, and that sooner or later he'd gain success. I think I told you my only regret is that I was not able to invest in his Pulitzer Prize winner. Cartwright had a large percentage of that play."

"Wait a minute. You mean to tell me that Cartwright was Benjy's angel *and* his shrink? That sounds strange to me, somehow."

Pamela Hudson was listening to our conversation intently. At last she spoke: "It certainly *does* sound strange, Hal. Dr. Cartwright never mentioned that relationship in any of our phone conversations. And it certainly isn't in his written summary of the case. I don't think I could treat a patient I had a business connection with."

"I assure you, Pam, that Charles is one of the outstanding

men in New York in his field. He has many clients in the
theater. Those people all seem to need some kind of help.
You'd be surprised at the famous names he has mentioned to
me. My God, he once recounted to me the awful problems
Josh Logan had. Unfortunately, it all came out when the poor
fellow passed away."

The conversation was beginning to be two-way between
the doctor and Mr. Denby. I figured it was time for me to slip
away.

"If you folks will excuse me," I said, "I'll be getting on
down to Monterey. The traffic this time of evening will be a
bitch, and I want to get home before supper time. It has been
a pleasure, Doctor. Nice seeing you again, Mr. Denby." I
shook hands with Pamela Hudson, then got a cold, clammy
clasp from Denby. As I left the lounge, I looked back and saw
Denby move closer to Dr. Hudson and place his hand over
hers on the table.

As I have said before, I have been extraordinarily lucky.
When I am working on a case, things seem to fall in my lap.
But the relationship of my client to the tall, beautiful shrink
was something I would have to look into. After all, there *was*
a Mrs. Denby in that big house on Jacks Peak. At least, there
was a handsome lady who always appeared in those society
page pictures clutching a highball glass.

And Hal Denby's connection to the murdered man was
beginning to take on some pretty interesting angles.
Cartwright, the New York psychiatrist, would bear some
examination. I was sure, however, that Denby wouldn't
finance a trip to Manhattan for me. I got the distinct feeling in
the cocktail lounge that he would have liked to fire me on the
spot. But he wouldn't. He'd have to explain that to Pamela
Hudson.

As I had anticipated, the traffic was nearly impossible
heading south from San Jose on Highway 101. I had chosen
that route rather than to head over the Santa Cruz Mountains
at the commute hour. Years of listening to a Bay Area news
radio station had told me that if there was going to be a drive

time collision or an overturned big rig, it would be on Highway 17 near the summit.

It was bumper to bumper on 101 for twenty miles. Then it began to loosen up south of Gilroy, and the run to the Monterey Peninsula was smooth. As soon as I cut over on the road to Castroville, heading west, the air outside began to cool down, and when I came to the junction of Highway One, I cut off my inefficient air conditioner and let the cool sea air pour in. Sometimes I wonder why I ever lived anyplace else. But that's what a hell of a lot of other people are thinking, and that ain't good. People are coming into Monterey, Pacific Grove, and Carmel in such great numbers that property prices have risen to astronomical heights. Yes, I said prices, not values. But it's whatever the traffic will bear, isn't it?

It was about quarter to seven when I rolled into Carmel, still light by virtue of Pacific Daylight Time. There were some thin wisps of fog beginning to blow in from the ocean and I knew it'd get heavier during the night. I pulled into my driveway feeling that it had been a confusing but generally profitable day.

The first thing I do when I get home is peek at my phone answering machine. I hate these things as much as Greg does, and have been known to leave smartass remarks on those of others, but Reiko badgered me to get this one. "Sometimes I can't find you for hours," she said. "And sometimes you pull out the plug on the phone so nobody can reach you. With this little device, you can get messages—and when a call comes in when you're here, you can listen and see if it's somebody you want to talk to."

I hit the button on the phone:

"Call me as soon as you hear this, goddamit." It was Reiko.

I continued to listen.

"Your pants are here at the Village Cleaners. We can't hold them much longer, Mr. Riordan."

"This is Leonard Elmore, Mr. Riordan. I'd like to give you a quote on your car insurance."

Each caller—except Reiko—gave a number. I wiped the tape and called her.

"It's about time. This you gotta know. Tak Oyama, my cousin that works at that hotel, remember? He knows the lady in the negligee that I saw in the room with Talbott. She was the one who was registered for the room, but under a different name. He had wondered about that, but in the hotel business, you don't ask too many questions. She's his wife, Riordan, she's Talbott's wife."

15
"Guess I blew it, huh?"

As ONE WHO, in his youth, had occasion to arrange clandestine meetings with women in hotels or motels, I can say with some authority that it is not customary for a red-blooded American male to schedule such an assignation with his own wife. Of course, I gave up that form of sport long before I met and married Helen. And I can say without fear of being struck by lightning that I was faithful to her to the end.

Braverman was right. There was a strong smell of fraud in the Talbott case.

"What's next, Riordan?" I could imagine Reiko twisting a lock of her short black hair and tapping her fingertips on the wall beside her phone.

"Can your cousin positively identify Mrs. Talbott?"

"Of course, dummy. He's seen her many times. Apparently she and her husband stayed at the hotel often when they used to visit from Sacramento. And Tak has a photographic memory."

"That still doesn't tell us much. Maybe the big guy who brought him to the hotel lifted him into the bed. Maybe he was making an effort to convince his wife that she should come back to him. You still didn't see him walk. Or demonstrate that he was capable of performing the *service* that his wife so passionately desires."

"I saw the look on her face, Riordan. That look, that flush, doesn't come from a kiss on the forehead."

"Sorry, little one. Congratulations on your perseverance and ingenuity, but we can't go to trial on your impressions. You didn't hang around and see if Talbott came out of the hotel?"

"No. I thought I had him. I was real pleased with myself. Guess I blew it, huh?"

"No, no, no, no. What you saw blows away a lot of the doubt. I was beginning to think I was wasting my time and yours, despite what Braverman said. But the Talbott case is taking on some very interesting aspects, and I want you to keep on it. Keep in touch with your cousin. Find out when and if Mrs. Talbott leaves the hotel. If possible, find out where she goes if she leaves. It's your baby, Reiko-san."

"Right, partner. See you in the morning."

"Forget about the office. Get out to the Talbott house first thing and see if anybody's there. Then check the hotel again. Did you get the name that the Talbott woman used to register?"

"Yeah. Funny thing. She signed herself Donna Mills. You know, she's an actress in on of those nighttime soap operas. One of my favorites, as a matter of fact."

"Does she look anything like Donna Mills? Hell, I'll take over the case myself if she does." I remembered the actress as Clint's little blonde cutie in *Play Misty For Me*.

"No, Riordan. She's just moderately pretty. You wouldn't whistle."

"I never whistle. Whatever you find out, call me. I'll be here or at the office or at . . ."

"Sally's office or Sally's condo. Want to leave any other numbers?"

"Go to bed. You can always leave a message on my infernal phone machine."

After I hung up I couldn't figure out why I had told Reiko to "go to bed." It was only about eight o'clock. And after the tedious drive down from San Jose, I had misplaced my sense of time. *And* I was sure as hell hungry.

There was nothing in my refrigerator but four TV dinners, an over-age carton of milk, several nectarines bought rock hard and left to ripen but now withered and showing fringes of fungus, half a dozen Snickers bars, and the carefully wrapped remains of a sandwich bought down at Bruno's either last week or the week before. On a shelf in one of the cabinets was half a bag of limp potato chips and a can of white clam chowder.

I walked down the hill and over to Bud's on Dolores. By this time of evening, the tourist crowd would have moved on, after discovering that Carmel shuts down tight at five-thirty. The sidewalks were relatively clear, and the air was cool. I had no trouble finding an empty table in the restaurant. They have a particularly good Shepherd's Pie there made with corned beef and I lost no time in ordering. I also ordered a bottle of Kaliber, a non-alcoholic beer made by the Guiness people that is my tipple of choice nowadays. Waitresses always give me a sidelong look when I ask for it. Somehow, you are suspect if you don't order booze in a place like Bud's.

I smiled at the girl winningly. "I'm a Druid by religion. We don't drink, you know."

"Oh, yes," she said. "I read that somewhere." But there was a look of doubt on her face..

Halfway through my meal I became aware of somebody standing over my table. I looked up to see a man of medium height with a red face that had been bloated, I judged, by an affection for very good Scotch, like the late Horace Stoneham, former owner of the Giants. He clutched a short glass of what I took to be his favorite beverage. His eyes were bloodshot and there was a faint smile on his face.

"You're Pat Riordan, aren't you?" He wasn't really asking. He knew damn' well who I was.

"I've seen you in court a couple of times, Riordan. You're pretty cool on the stand, you know that?"

I looked hard at the guy. After all, my Shepherd's Pie was getting cold. He did seem familiar.

"I'm Nick Costa, attorney for Talbott. You've been snooping around my client's house. Working for the insurance company, eh?"

Costa was a little drunk. Not like falling down or anything like that. The light behind those beady eyes was on high beam. He swayed just a little as he stood too close to my table.

"Sit down, Costa. Before you bump into my table and knock my food on the floor."

He lowered his bulk into a chair opposite me and put down his glass with great care. His face was oily and shone even in the subdued light of the restaurant. His hair, iron gray, was plastered against his head with some kind of evil smelling pomade.

"My client is severely handicapped, Riordan, and deserves generous compensation. He is unable to walk, and now even his, ah, sexual function is impaired."

"Yeah, I understand he cannot rise to the challenge any more."

"Exactly. For this reason, his beloved wife, otherwise a truly saintly person, has left him. A woman has needs, you know."

"I know. But this saintly cookie must not have had much deep affection for her husband if she runs out on him when he has been rendered helpless after his accident."

Costa shrugged. "Who knows about these things? I feel that she genuinely loves the man. But the idea of spending her entire life with a man who can't. . . . You must understand that Mrs. Talbott is in her early thirties."

"OK, counselor. She has my deepest sympathy. Now can I eat my dinner?"

Costa didn't move. "Riordan, I must ask you to stop harassing my client. He is a man of delicate sensibilities and is

being made extremely nervous by your surveillance. You're
not very good at surveillance, are you Riordan?"

Now, this was a bloody insult, by God. I have always
prided myself on my uncanny ability to tail a suspect's car or
follow an errant husband on foot to the dwelling of his mis-
tress.

"Whaddaya mean, extremely nervous? What's this guy got
to be nervous about. He's got this big bodyguard. Or is it a
practical nurse? Carries him around like a baby."

Costa appeared to look surprised. Or he put on a pretty
good act, I wasn't sure at the time. "Bodyguard? There's no
one else living at Talbott's house. He manages by himself,
with the help of a visiting nursing service that also supplies
somebody to tidy up now and then. We've had his bathroom
furnished with helpful appliances, and he can swing himself
off the bed into the wheelchair without assistance. The man is
remarkable. I see him frequently, and I'm amazed at what he
can do without the use of his lower body. Bodyguard? I have
no idea what or who you have in mind."

16
"Fat bastard. . . ."

I HAD NEVER met Nick Costa before, even though I was aware of his reputation and had seen him, as he had seen me, only in court on two or three occasions. He was an enormously successful criminal lawyer who would skate pretty close to the edge in defending a client. Nobody would accuse him out loud of dishonesty in his practice, but I knew a lot of attorneys who had come out of a courtroom muttering to themselves after losing a case to Costa. Words like "asshole," and "disbarment."

His reaction to my mention of the big man who carried Charles Talbott to his car and escorted him to the hotel to meet his "estranged" wife was carefully calculated to appear genuine. Drunks are usually incapable of subtlety. You scare a drunk, he looks scared. You surprise him, he shows it. Costa appeared to be surprised. The only reason I could think of at the time was that Talbott was conning his lawyer as well as everybody else. On the other hand, I thought that Costa would be a tough guy to con.

"Counselor, are you aware that poor old Charlie Talbott

has a history of litigation with insurance companies? That he accepted very substantial settlements resulting from accident claims in Nebraska and Ohio? And those are the only ones the people I represent have found out about. The curious thing that connects the dots is that all the claims have come from accidents involving very large trucking companies. Now why do you suppose that good old Charlie always mixes it up with big interstate trucks? And how do you account for the fact that in the other two known incidents, he recovered miraculously after being partially paralyzed?"

Costa had moved pretty close to me and his drink was spilling into my lap. He stood up shakily and backed away, colliding with a waitress carrying a plate of pasta, and went down hard on his more than ample rump. A busboy and two nearby diners helped the man to his feet. He looked at me blankly, made an effort to remove festoons of fettuccini from his coat tail, and, with as much dignity as he could muster, lumbered from the room.

The excitement didn't last long. I think crowds of locals in Carmel are pretty blasé. The people around me resumed eating and drinking. The only reminder of the incident was the busboy cleaning up the spilled noodles and aromatic pesto sauce.

"Fat bastard," I heard the kid say under his breath.

"You've met this guy before?" I asked. "He's had other collisions, spilled other messy foodstuffs?"

"Hell, I never saw the sonofabitch until tonight. But I've met a lot like him. This is my first night in this joint."

That little warning light in my head began to blink, and I took a closer look at the young man. He was tall and thin, with a terrible case of acne, narrow eyes, and a sullen mouth. "Sean Wetherby?"

The kid looked up at me sharply. "How'd you know my name?"

"Just instinct. Na-a-ah. We met before, my friend. At the Forest Theater. The rehearsal, remember? I'm a friend of Sally Morse."

"Oh, yeah. The private dick. So who killed the little faggot? Any idea?"

I hadn't been called a "dick" in that sense in many a year.

"That's the second time I have heard Benjy Noble referred to as a homosexual. Do you have evidence to the fact that the allegation is true?"

"He never made a pass at me, if that's what you mean. But I saw him hanging around the beach a lot, and he wasn't lookin' at the girls."

The maître d' drew near, sternly and wordlessly indicating that Sean should get on with his cleanup and get the hell back to work. He smiled at me. "Everything all right, sir?"

"Sure, if you'll get me a dry pair of shorts. I got a jar of Chivas Regal in my lap."

The man flushed. "Oh, I'm sorry, sir. Boy, get a couple of fresh napkins and help this customer. I didn't realize, sir, that anything got spilled on you. Mr. Costa has fallen in here on other occasions, but usually it's been damaging only to the help."

The "boy" gave the man a venomous glare, grabbed a napkin off an empty table, tossed it into my lap, and was about to stalk off.

"Wait, Sean," I said. "What time do you get off work?"

He looked at me suspiciously. "Hey, maybe *you're* the faggot."

"You could call Sally, kid. No, I'd just like to talk to you about your hassles with Noble. You and he didn't get along, right?"

"Damn right. I couldn't stand the little fairy. And what he wrote was a lot of shit."

"Look, when you get off here, come on up to my place. I guarantee I won't lay a hand on you. I'd just like to get your angle on Noble's death. You ever own a Swiss army knife?"

"I didn't kill him. I would like to have killed him, but I don't have the guts, detective. Everybody knows what a gutless wonder I am. My parents don't recognize me on the street."

"Will you come up? It's the old cottage at the southwest corner of Sixth and Santa Rita. When you get off."

"OK." The maître d' was hovering again, so the kid picked up his mess and headed for the kitchen.

Either Sean Wetherby was a consummate actor—which I doubted—or he was entirely innocent of Benjy Noble's murder. I finished my meal, paid my check, and tried to leave the restaurant inconspicuously with a red napkin tucked into my belt and hanging down like Tarzan's loincloth. "I'll return this in a day or so," I said to the host as I passed him. "It is not etiquette in Carmel to wet one's pants in an eating place."

I didn't attract much attention winding up Sixth Avenue to my place. The tourists still abroad probably thought I was a local eccentric who always dressed with a red napkin hanging from his belt. The residents probably thought I was a tourist who had embraced a new trend in vacation wear.

Anyhow, after puffing up the hill to Santa Rita, I sat down in my well-worn recliner and pointed my remote device at the TV. Funny things were happening in a Boston bar. A bit later there was a thing about a fashionable Los Angeles law firm, consisting of glamorously unreal attorneys, whose personal adventures were more interesting than the cases they handled. At about eleven o'clock, there was a knock at my door.

I clicked off the television and admitted Sean Wetherby. He was wearing his restaurant clothes and smelled of garlic and dishwater. I directed him to the couch near the fireplace. He sat down at one end, and I took a position at the other.

"In case you've forgotten, Sean, my name is Pat Riordan. Just so you'll have something to call me. What I want is your own story of your relationship with Benjy Noble, and anything else you happen to think of about the involvement of other people who just might have had some sort of motive for killing him."

"Like I told you, Riordan, I didn't kill him. I did like the touch with the knife. Wish to hell I could have seen it. The little bastard with the red handle of a Swiss army knife stickin' out of his throat. What a great picture."

"You and he didn't get along, though, right?"

"I couldn't stand him. From the beginning. We were in Hal Denby's dining room for five days before we were going to take the play on the stage for blocking. He wrote such garbage for all of us. I was the only one who bitched about it. The rest of them were just sheep. Sorry, but your girl friend was as big a sheep as the others. This guy may have won a lot of prizes, but he wrote garbage."

"Why didn't you quit?"

"I'm an actor. And an actor at this level doesn't have the opportunity to be choosy, especially if a lot of people insist that the play is important, and it gets a lot of publicity."

"I thought you were a busboy."

He bristled. "You don't know a helluva lot, do you? Actors can't take regular jobs. They've got to be available. The only jobs I take are ones I can quit without notice."

I took a long look at the "actor." The kid, whose garlicky aroma was suffocating from five feet away, was relaxed and self-possessed. If he was the least bit nervous, he didn't show it.

"Sean, if you didn't kill Noble, do you have any notion of who might have done it? Anybody with a big enough hate?"

He thought a moment and then smiled. "Your girl friend was too impressed by the bastard to get mad at him. Cordelia is a little-old-lady type. Temp Hedges is a no-talent. He peddles stocks to little old ladies like Cordelia. But Christy. . . ." His smile broadened. "You remember Christy—the little girl with the big tits? Well, Christy tried to put the make on Benjy from the beginning. She's a show biz veteran, Riordan, if you count the casting couch. How she got the part, I don't know. She had the looks for it, I guess. But when she tried to get Benjy to turn on, he just ignored her. This she couldn't understand. It never occurred to her that Benjy preferred boys. And she got pretty uptight. She never said anything . . . but I've known her a long time. I can't say she's ever killed anybody. But she sure as hell can be dangerous. And I've got a couple of scars to prove it."

17
"What is it about Cordelia?"

WHEN SEAN left a bit later I pressed a twenty-dollar bill into his hand. I felt sort of guilty for having suspected the kid. My instinct was that he could get mad as hell, and maybe hit somebody with a stick, but could not generate the fury necessary to batter a human being the way Benjy Noble had been battered. Neither was he capable of decorating the body with an elaborate pocket knife. That took a joker with a truly twisted mind. A man—or a woman—who was crazy enough to pull the little plastic toothpick out of the knife and lodge it between the victim's front teeth.

Before he left, I got Sean to tell me where to find Christy Burgess.

"She works in one of those high-fashion, high-price shops in the Plaza," he told me. "She likes to strut around in those fancy clothes. And she gets guys to buy 'em for her. The one tragedy in her life is that she never got tall enough to be a model. She wears these real high spike heels so she can look taller than she is. But it doesn't do much good. She lives in a little one-room apartment in one of those alleys between San

Carlos and Mission. I know it's upstairs, but I'm not sure just where. I could never get to first base with her, although I know from some of my friends that she was a real easy lay. *If* a guy was a big spender."

Next morning, I called the office fairly early, about the time Reiko would ordinarily get in. When the phone rang four times and the machine cut in, I hung up. I gave up after trying several times more at ten minute intervals, listened to my own mellifluous tones on the machine inviting the caller to leave a message at the tone, and left a message: "Where the hell are you? I'll be in around noon. Write if you get work."

At ten or so I wandered down the hill to the Carmel Plaza, a complex of trendy retail establishments that has been blessed by the tour bus companies as the first stop for the crowds that arrive daily during the summer. Sean had been a little vague about which shop Christy worked in, so I had to poke my head in and look around half a dozen of them until I spotted her.

Business is pretty light at opening time. Lots of the tourists are just having breakfast. Some of them might still be in bed, although what might have kept them up late I cannot imagine. In Carmel after about five-thirty, you can eat, you can drink if you want to, you can go to the movies, or on weekends you can take in whatever is playing at the Forest Theater. What the people do who have babes in arms and kids in strollers (many have both), I have no idea. You can sit in a motel room and watch TV. But most Carmel motels and hotels won't take kids under twelve or so. At ten in the morning the buses haven't begun to arrive. So when I spotted her, Christy Burgess was languidly straightening out some over-priced dresses hanging on a rack in the back of the store.

As I approached, she pulled a dress off the rack and stood in front of a mirror, as women will, with the dress draped over her, contemplating the image with obvious approval. When she became aware of me, she turned on a wide smile that revealed a set of glistening white teeth that were obviously her own.

"Mr. Riordan . . . the detective. I knew you'd look me up. I could tell by the way you held my hand when we met. Is there something special you'd like to see?" Her voice was full of promise and suggestion. Yeah, I thought, I'd like to see this little tramp in a bikini. But business is business.

"Actually, Christy, I'm just asking a few questions of all the people who had contact with Benjy Noble since he arrived in Carmel. For my information, you understand. Somebody in the cast of *Waiting for the L-Train* might have knowledge of something or other to help us find out who might have wanted Benjy dead. How about you?"

Her smile didn't flicker. She hung up the dress she still had draped over her shoulder and took my hand. "I'll be free for lunch at one. I . . . really can't take time out from my work. And I'm sure we could find other things to talk about besides Benjy Noble. He was a dear, sweet man and I feel awful about what happened to him, but I knew him such a short time."

There wasn't a hell of a lot I could do. I told Christy I'd pick her up at one o'clock and went on my way. Around the corner on Mission I stopped at a pay phone and called the office again. Again, no Reiko. I began to wonder if she was sick. I called her apartment, but got no answer there. Goddamit, I thought, where is she? Ordinarily, I don't worry too much about Reiko. She's made of steel and grit and can handle herself in any situation. I shrugged it off. But I felt a little uneasy.

With nothing much to occupy me until one, I walked up the long Junipero Street hill to the police station. The policewoman at the front desk, who is also the dispatcher, sent me into John Miller's office. "I won't announce you, Mr. Riordan. Lieutenant Miller gets mad at me if I ring his phone when he's doing reports. But he won't get mad at you for interrupting him. He's always looking for an excuse to get out of paperwork."

Miller was absorbed in his work and swearing softly when I walked up to his desk. He looked up at me and asked, "Do you have to do any of this stuff, Pat? Do you have to fill out forms with all sorts of irrelevant horseshit because the forms are there to fill out. No. You don't. Reiko does all the work, doesn't she?"

"She does not do all the work, John. It's just that I cannot type . . . and I certainly cannot operate that electronic apparatus that she has so much faith in. So she does the letters and reports and such. I do most of the thinking. Reiko is a worker. I am a thinker."

Miller sat back and smirked. "If you were not basically honest, you'd be the most successful con man in California, perhaps in the forty-eight contiguous states. You could probably make it in Hawaii, but I can't see you in one of those wild shirts. Alaska is out. I'd judge you can't think in cold weather."

"OK. Now that you've insulted me, you owe me a little something. What's new in the Benjy Noble case?"

"Very little. You know about the lady on the hill who *heard* something. You know about the psychiatrist in San Jose and the other shrink in New York. Incidentally, he's flying to San Francisco in a couple of days for a meeting, so we'll get a chance to talk to him. You know about Cordelia Pompilio—"

"Hold it. What is it about Cordelia? She's older than she looks and she's got phony red hair, that I know. What else? I saw her once and she didn't say anything when we met. She was in the rehearsal that I watched. She has a voice that won't get past the second row. What does she have to do with Noble?"

"She's his aunt. Nobody knew that until she whispered it in Harold Denby's ear yesterday at a cast meeting. She's Noble's father's sister. Been living on the Peninsula for twenty years."

"Have you questioned her?"

"No, not yet. She claimed the body yesterday as Noble's only living relative. She's arranging for what she calls the 'disposal of the remains.'"

"How many more interested parties are going to emerge from the bushes?"

"Oh, hell, Riordan, you know how these things are. The only person we're sure didn't commit the murder is good old Abe Atterbury, who confessed to the job. Only he claims he did it in a religious frenzy with a scimitar."

I told Miller about my conference with Sean Wetherby and my imminent date with Christy Burgess.

"We've talked to both of them. It's my opinion that neither one is a killer, although they ain't too bright. But, remember, Patrick, if you get *anything* that seems significant, I better damn' well hear about it right away."

I reassured Miller, and went on my way. There was still about an hour to kill when I left the police station, so I stopped by my house. Further calls to the office and to Reiko's apartment were fruitless. I caught a noon newscast on Channel 36, and drank a Diet 7-Up. Not much was new. Midsummer newscasts are a lot like summer newspapers: they contain a lot of talking dog· stories and pictures of pretty semi-nude girls sitting on ice cakes. I damn' near fell asleep.

At ten to one I walked down the hill to the Plaza. Christy was waiting for me at the front door of her shop.

"Where to, kid?" I asked.

She gave me that smile that must have made her dentist proud. "I do love Guglielmo's," she said, naming one of the most expensive places in town. I felt my money clip and tried to gauge the amount. If there were some tens and twenties, I was all right.

As we walked up the hill, Christy took my arm in a warm, familiar grip. I hoped to God I wouldn't run into Sally Morse. We were ushered into the restaurant by an obsequious host-person (a designation I deplore), and seated in a corner away from the front windows. I think I just wasn't the type the management wanted potential customers to see from the outside.

The place is quite small, and if it had been crowded I would have been elbow to elbow with a total stranger. But it isn't really a tourist trap, and there was only a handful of people, mostly locals it seemed.

Christy clasped my hand tightly when we were seated side

by side on a banquette. I have never felt such a hot little hand in all my career of holding hands with girls.

She slid as close to me as she could get, pinning me against the wall. I felt the room get very warm indeed.

"Will you excuse me just a moment, Christy? I have to make a very important phone call."

At the moment, I think I was just trying to escape. But there was something else. Try as I might, I couldn't forget about Reiko. The host-person reluctantly led me to a phone in the back of the room.

I tried the apartment first. No response. Then I called the office. A familiar voice—not Reiko's—answered the phone.

"Who the hell is this?" I asked.

"Pat? Tony Balestreri. I came looking for you. Couldn't get you on the telephone. Guess I'm guilty of breaking and entering, but that office door of yours is . . ."

"What is it?" I was alarmed, really alarmed.

"Take it easy. She's going to be all right."

"*Who's* going to be all right? What are you talking about?"

"It's Reiko, Pat. She's up at Community Hospital. She's been shot."

18
"She's still in emergency."

I'VE LIVED MORE than half a century, and I've gone
through a lot of heavy weather, but nothing ever shocked me
so much as hearing that Reiko had been shot. I forgot about
everything: Benjy Noble, Charlie Talbott, Harold Denby—
everything. I especially forgot about Christy Burgess. Until I
was rushing through the restaurant to the front door. I
stopped long enough to pull a couple of twenties out of my
money clip and toss them on the table. "Eat hearty," I said.
"Catch you next time."

Christy obviously wasn't used to being dumped unceremo-
niously, and she sat there with her eyes wide and her mouth
open. I ran out of the restaurant and up the hill to get my car.

I've told you that the climb up Sixth Avenue to my house
is very steep, and that I get winded just thinking about it. Not
this time. I felt no strain at all as I galloped up the slope, and I
was on Carpenter Street heading out of town five minutes
after I left the restaurant.

Tony Balestreri is a sergeant in the Sheriff's Department.
We've been close friends ever since I came to the Monterey

Peninsula. When he reassured me that Reiko was going to be all right, I believed him. But the adrenaline that was pumping inside me did not subside. I think I could have been cited for at least four traffic violations on the trip up to the Community Hospital. When I arrived, I parked in an ambulance zone, ignored the shout of a security guard, and ran through the automatic gurney doors almost before they opened.

Balestreri was waiting for me. "I just got here myself. How the hell did you make it so fast? I got the notion you were in a restaurant or something."

"Where is she, Tony?"

"She's still in emergency. They've got a bit of repair work to do. The bullet went through the right side of the lower abdomen and nicked the large intestine. Chipped the hipbone just a tad. But it was a clean wound, and there's no permanent damage. She'll be laid up for maybe a month, but . . ."

"Can I see her?"

"In an hour or so. She's still anesthetized. But these guys are very good at what they do. Come on over here and sit down."

"My car. I've got to move my car." I could see the security guard bearing down on me.

"Don't worry, I'll fix it." Balestreri intercepted the guard and spoke to him in a low voice. He came back to me. "Your keys, Pat." I still had them in my hand, so I handed them over without question. The Sergeant passed the keys to the guard, and returned to me.

"He'll see that your car is parked. Then he'll come back here and tell us where it is and bring your keys back. They're pretty good about those things here."

"What happened, Tony?"

"First, you tell me what Reiko was doing out on Jacks Peak. When my people found her, she was walking down Loma Alta in a daze, holding her side, pale as a ghost. We found her car about a hundred yards from where we found her. We were goddam lucky—or *she* was goddam lucky. If we hadn't had a cruiser up in the neighborhood, she might be there yet, and. . . ."

"Don't say it. Thanks, Tony. And thanks to your guy who found her. God knows what she was doing up on the Peak. I've had her on a surveillance assignment for an insurance company. A guy the company thinks is a faker with a million-dollar suit. She'll have to tell us what took her up the hill. Last I heard, she was checking out the guy's residence, or maybe the hotel where his wife was staying, or . . ."

"Never mind. If it's not in my jurisdiction, I don't want to know about it."

Balestreri left me with a comforting hand on the shoulder, telling me quietly to stay in touch and call him when I had had the chance to talk to Reiko. I waited in that emergency ward forever. I almost asked somebody for a cigarette, something I had forsworn for twenty years. I tried to read a magazine, but found myself stuck in one paragraph of an article on atherosclerosis which I read over and over, hoping I could understand it.

Eventually, a nurse approached. "Mr. Riordan? Miss Masuda is awake now. You can see her for just a few minutes."

She led me down the hall to a room containing two beds, on one of which was the small form of my beloved partner. She had her eyes closed when I moved quietly up to her bedside. I swear to God she looked about ten years old, and I felt my eyes filling up.

"A fine mess you got me into, you sonofabitch," she said as she opened one eye.

I bent down and kissed her on the cheek, and she put one arm limply around my neck.

Then she went to sleep.

19
I was in a kind of stupor.

I SAT BY the hospital bed for two hours, watching Reiko sleep. She had an IV in her right arm, and a drainage tube threaded through her nose down into her stomach to keep it clear until the repair of the intestine could heal properly. It all looked terribly uncomfortable, but she slept like a baby—and looked like one. When it became obvious to me that she was probably going to be out for a long time, I slipped out the door.

My car was down the hill in the visitors' parking lot. Community Hospital is on a ridge that runs along the crest of a hill between Monterey and Pebble Beach. It looks like a country club, and I've often thought that if anybody has to be sick, this is sure as hell the place to do it. An extraordinary place to die, for sure. But no matter how often they increase the size of the parking lot, it still doesn't seem to be enough. And unless they do something about the narrow road leading up from Highway One on the east and Pacific Grove on the west, people are going to die in the ambulances during peak traffic hours. A siren can do a hell of a lot of screeching, but if there's no room on the road to get through, that's it.

I was in a kind of stupor. There was no way I could accept the fact that Reiko had been shot—on a job that I pushed her into. *And* there was no reason that a routine surveillance on a fraud case should wind up with a bullet in the gut. But Reiko was the only one who had the details, and I couldn't talk to her yet. It was late in the afternoon when I drove down into Monterey.

My office seemed strangely cold. I had a hollow feeling as I passed Reiko's desk, with its exotic computer components creeping in all directions. Sitting at my own scarred and barren desk, I tried to get my brain in gear.

It's hard for people to accept that a man in my business doesn't carry a gun, or even have one tucked in a desk drawer. I try to explain that I was an infantry Pfc. in Korea, and after months of trading small arms fire with an enemy that was trying to kill me for no good reason, after months of seeing good buddies and replacements I had known for maybe a few hours go down with holes in them, I swore I'd never touch a gun again in my life. Once or twice I've had to renege on that oath. There were unexpected occasions when somebody shoved a piece in my hand. But I don't own one, and God knows I don't carry one. And Reiko—she wouldn't know a handgun from a shotgun.

I don't know how long I sat at my desk in the gathering shadows. It was pretty dark when I realized that I hadn't turned on the lights, and the street below me had quieted down from the heavy traffic of the business day. I switched on my desk lamp and looked at my watch. This is a more complicated process than it sounds. I cannot read my watch without the little half-glasses I carry in my breast pocket. My eye doctor insists that I need bifocals, but something inside me will not surrender to creeping old age. Anyhow, it was seven-thirty. I called Sally at home.

When I told her about Reiko, she was genuinely shocked. As I've said before, Sally and Reiko are not the best of friends. Oh, they have a healthy respect for each other, but they probably would never go shopping together. I like to think that each is jealous of the other because of me. I like to think that, even if it's not true. Probably each is jealous of the other's independence. They're rivals, competitors in a new society. I'm stuck with a pre-WW II culture. I was seven years old when it started, and became very much aware of it. Sally is older than Reiko, but both of them were post-war babies. Although there isn't quite a full generation that separates me from them (and I hate to use the word "yuppie"), Sally and Reiko operate under a different set of rules.

"How did it happen?" Sally's voice was tense.

"That's just it. I don't know. She's the only one who knows, and she's out of it, probably until tomorrow morning."

"Didn't you know you were exposing her to danger? How could you send Reiko out on a job you should have done yourself?" She was angry. Just what I *didn't* need.

"Hold it, Sal. It was a routine fraud investigation. No worse than a divorce surveillance. All she had to do was check out this guy to see if he's faking an injury in a lawsuit. Piece of cake—usually. I cannot imagine why there would be gunplay."

That seemed to placate her. "I'm sorry, Pat. I know we're not special friends, but I do *like* Reiko. It's just that she's a little . . . snippy, sometimes. But I guess I'm not all sweetness and light. What are you going to do tonight? Want to come out here?"

That was an offer I could not refuse. It wasn't that I was horny, you understand. I don't think I could have made love if Kim Basinger had been standing naked in front of me. But I needed somebody to talk to. And Sally always listens.

She has ignored me often, but she listens.

When I got to Sally's condo, she scrambled up a batch of eggs with bacon and potatoes (a massive dose of cholesterol—but I didn't complain), and I began to relax. Thoughts of my investigation of Benjy Noble's murder crept back into my consciousness.

"Sal, how well do you know the other people in the cast of *Waiting for the L-Train?*"

"Some better than others." She looked thoughtful. "Cordelia used to be a neighbor here until she bought a small house in Carmel. Said she felt isolated in the Valley and was afraid to drive the Valley road. I've known her maybe six or seven years, but not that well. The little sexpot, Christy, used to wait on me at Magnin's, but she's working someplace else now. All I know about her is all anybody needs to know about Christy. She'll keep casting until she lands a big fish. And she certainly has the bait. Sean Wetherby is the most talented person in the crowd. I've seen him do a lot of very good minor bits in shows around the county. But I understand he's a strange, moody kid. His parents have used my agency for European tours. They're super straight. I guess I've known Temp Hedges longer than any of the others. He used to come around when I was first married, trying to get Jimmy to invest a chunk of money he'd got for writing a movie score. But you know Jimmy. He never put a dime away."

I *didn't* know Jimmy Morse, except that he had been married to Sally back in the sixties when they were both very young. He's a trumpet player, probably a very talented one, but more than a little unstable. He comes around now and then. He's a studio musician in Hollywood, and Sally sort of mothers him. But she's always made it a point to keep him away from me. And I don't ask questions.

"What else do you know about Hedges? He came around to the office and tried to sell me on his idea that Sean might be the killer."

"I don't think so, Pat. True, from what I've heard, Sean can get pretty violent. Fights in bars and all that. And I know that he and Benjy didn't get along. But I really don't think he could have waylaid Benjy at the theater and beat him to death. Then that awful thing with the knife. . . ."

"What about Hedges himself? Any possibility that he could have done the job?"

Sally laughed. "The wimp with the old-fashioned mustache? You've got to be kidding. This guy lives in mortal fear of his *wife*. He's probably afraid of the dark. And he's a rotten actor."

I wasn't sure what being a "rotten actor" had to do with Templeton Hedges' being a potential killer. But I was willing to take Sally's word for it. And suddenly, I realized how tired I was. My bones ached.

"Sal, do you mind if I spend the night? I am completely bushed. I could sleep on the couch."

"Don't be an idiot, Riordan. Go on in the bedroom. I promise not to touch you. I'm going to stay up for 'thirtysomething'."

I couldn't resist. "I thought you were more like 'forty-something'."

She whacked me on the butt pretty hard. I stumbled into the bedroom, and was asleep almost before I could get my clothes off.

20

It was too nice a day to feel guilty.

IN A startling role reversal, Sally was shaking me awake the next morning. I don't think I had ever slept quite so soundly as I did that night. It was exhaustion, I guess, but something else, too. The good Dr. Hudson of San Jose would no doubt tell me that I was trying to escape the guilt I felt about Reiko.

"Smell the coffee, Pat. It's pushing eight-thirty and I have to be in my office in a half hour. Somebody might want to go somewhere. Wake up, dammit."

I emerged slowly into the bright daylight. It's usually foggy in Carmel on a summer morning, but in the Valley the sun appears early, and begins to heat things up right away. I climbed out of bed in my underwear. I hate to sleep in my underwear, but I hadn't had the energy to get into the yellow nightshirt I keep at Sally's.

"Go on. Get out. I am not at my best. Go to your office and send the entire population on a guided tour of Mandalay, if you want to. My hair is wild, my beard is scratchy, and my breath is probably bad. So go."

Sally kissed me lightly on the lips. "It's not so bad. I didn't put any onions in that mess I cooked for you. But you better get up and get over to the hospital. Reiko's probably conscious by now."

The guilt descended on me again, and I felt rotten. I dressed hastily and brushed my teeth as Sally's car was pulling out of the carport. I thought briefly of trying to hide my beard with Sally's pancake makeup, but dismissed the idea as mildly insane. I would simply appear at the hospital with a stubble on my jaw and hope that people would mistake me for a movie star.

It was too nice a day to feel guilty. My spirits began to lift as I drove west on the Valley road. After all, Reiko was recovering. I could have lost her. But she was probably hurting pretty bad. The guilt came back. But how could I have known that somebody would pull a gun on her? And who the hell could it have been?"

There was plenty of room in the parking lot at the hospital when I arrived. I walked up the hill enjoying the sparkling morning and breathing the fresh ocean breeze. I was feeling less like a careless, callous bastard. However, when I opened the door to Reiko's room, I was back to square one. I couldn't count 'em all at a glance, but it seemed as if her entire family had gathered around her bed. Her mother had arrived from Willow Glen, and was staring daggers at me. Uncle Shiro, who owns the building our office is in, projected a furious glare at me. The other assorted cousins and such looked like so many avenging samurai, even the women.

"Hi, Pat, come on in," said Reiko, smiling as brightly as possible with a tube coming out of her nose. "You know most of these people, don't you?"

I nodded dumbly at the visitors. I was honestly thinking about getting out of the room in a hurry, but I decided to tough it out.

"Mrs. Masuda. Shiro. Virgil, Emma." I tried to remember the other names without success. Most of Reiko's cousins go by Anglo names like Derek and Kevin, et cetera. I was smiling now, but still pretty wary.

"They were just leaving, weren't you, Mama? You just go on out to my apartment. Uncle Shiro has the key. You can come back to see me this evening. Go, now, Mama. I have to talk to Pat."

I pressed up against the wall as the group moved slowy by me. Not one of them said a word. But their eyes said plenty.

"They'll get over it, Riordan," said Reiko as the last of the relatives cleared the door. "It's just such a shock to them. Mama just cried and said that this wasn't what she sent me to San Jose State for. She kept asking me why I didn't get a teaching credential. I told her that since Grampa had left us all that money, I was going to do something exciting. Getting shot was exciting. Sure a lot more exciting than sitting at that damn' desk in that damn' office."

Reiko's grandfather had come out of a World War II detention camp and set out to regain all the property that he had lost. He succeeded in acquiring orchard and farm land in what later became the heart of Silicon Valley. At the proper moment, he sold off the property for a staggering profit and retired to a small bonsai business. When he died, he left his family financially independent. That's the only reason Reiko came to work for me in the first place. She didn't need the money. And I didn't have it.

"You want to know what happened? OK. Sit down, make yourself comfortable. I'll tell you." She took my hand. "Don't feel bad, Pat. I'm going to be all right. It's kind of my own fault, anyhow. I guess I stuck my neck out."

I was finally able to speak. "Reiko-san, I am truly sorry I got you into something like this. I had no idea. . . ."

"Shut up, will you, and listen to what I have to say. OK?" She frowned and dug her nails into my palm.

"After I talked to you—when I told you about the lady in the hotel being Talbott's wife—I went to bed, like you told me. But something kept me awake. Along about three in the morning, it finally dawned on me what it was. The big guy who carried Talbott out of the house and pushed him in the wheelchair at the hotel. I had seen him someplace before. And

it wasn't in church or at the movies. I had seen him in a courtroom. Remember when I used to go over to Salinas to watch
Howard Gravesend try cases? Before Howard was killed, you
know. God, he was slick in court. Too bad he was so dumb
otherwise."

It *had* to be before Howard was killed, honey, I thought.
He was sort of handicapped after. Gravesend's death had pre-
cipitated a lot of crazy things a while back, but that's another
story.

Reiko went on. "The big guy—his name was Kozinsky, or
something like that—was up on a charge of attempted homicide and Howard was defending him. In the beginning it
looked like he didn't have a chance. But, by the time
Gravesend got through with that jury, they were ready to give
the big guy a medal. They decided that he had been provoked
beyond endurance, and acquitted him. Kozinsky, or whatever,
didn't say 'thank you' or even shake hands with Howard. He
just walked out of the courtroom through the crowd all by
himself. But I remember him, clear as day.

"Well, the morning after I talked to you and remembered
him, I went back to the Talbott house. You know me,
Riordan. I'm pretty direct. I knocked on the door. No answer.
I even walked around and looked in the windows. Not a soul
in the place.

"So, I went on downtown to the hotel. Just as I pulled up
across the street, here comes this big gorilla wheeling Talbott
out to his car. And I think they're going back home. They
head up Calle Principal, so I follow them. But pretty soon
we're on Aguajito Road on the way up into the woods this
side of Jacks Peak. The car turns into one of those long private driveways so I can't follow them without being noticed.
So I park and walk. When the car stops in front of the house,
both of these men—Kozinsky and Talbott—get out as big as
you please and walk up to the front steps. I guess I made
some sort of noise, because the big guy turns and comes in my
direction with a gun in his hand. I took off through the woods
towards Loma Alta, but he came after me pretty fast. Then,

all of a sudden, something bangs into me, and at the same time, I hear a shot. I must have been knocked out for a second because the next thing I knew, I was in this little hole, behind a tree.

"I'm aware of the big guy tramping through the woods not far away. So I just curl up and play dead. He finally gives up looking and, I guess, goes back to the house. But his time, my belly is beginning to hurt pretty bad. I'm bleeding. But the only thing I can think of is to get the hell out of that place as quickly as possible. So when I thought it was safe to move, I walked down the hill. I was dazed, I guess. All I could think of was getting back to the office. I even walked past my car. The only thing I can remember is a name that was on one of those country mail boxes right by the private driveway."

"What was it, Reiko-san? What was the name?"

"It was a short name. I can remember it because it was short. Costa. That was it. Costa."

21
"We were so proud of him."

WHEN NICK COSTA fell into the fettuccine in Bud's, I had got the impression that he was genuinely surprised about the existence of Charlie Talbott's "bodyguard." My impression seemed to be substantiated by Costa's loss of equilibrium when I confronted him with the facts about Talbott's record of litigation. But the name Costa on a mailbox near where somebody shot Reiko. . . . Had to be the same guy. How many Costas could Talbott be hooked up with? And how did this guy Kozinski fit in?

Reiko had fallen silent for a moment. She seemed very tired, probably from answering a lot of questions from the gaggle of relatives which had descended on her that morning. She lay back and closed her eyes.

"I'm sorry," she said. "I can't remember much more. I was walking down that road. I saw the sheriff's car. A man got out and ran up to me. Then he picked me up and put me in the car. Next thing I knew, I was here and a lot of people were swarming over me. It's beginning to hurt, Pat. Something must be wearing off."

She seemed to want to sleep, but the pain was keeping her awake. I walked out into the hall and signalled the nurse's desk.

"Can you give her a shot or something? She seems to be hurting considerably." The nurse gave me one of those nurse-like looks that said, "Just leave the professional work to us, mister." But she checked Reiko's chart and came back with a syringe. In a few minutes, my fallen partner slipped into a peaceful slumber. I tiptoed out of the room.

Before I left the hospital I called Tony Balestreri.

"What do you know about a big ugly guy named Kozinsky? Haven't got a first name. Ring any bells?"

"Eddie Kozinsky. A small-timer with a big body. He has a very colorful record in the county. Several ADW counts, as I recall, but he always seems to get off. Your old buddy Howard Gravesend used to defend him. Gravesend did magic in the courtroom. *If* that's the guy you're talking about."

"It fits." I told him about the Talbott case and its sexy ramifications, about the involvement of Kozinsky and Nick Costa, and the fact that Reiko had identified Kozinsky as the man who shot her.

"Whew. I've never heard of Costa getting involved in this kind of thing. Sure, he has cut a few corners now and then, and he's pretty generally disliked in the legal profession, but he has covered his ass very well. Not like him to have a hand in a clearly fraudulent case. I wouldn't trust him, Pat, but if I were in trouble, I'd want him to defend me. Since Gravesend is gone. But what can I do about Kozinsky?"

"You could pick the bastard up."

"I could pick him up and he'd be out in a couple of hours. Reiko says it was Kozinsky who shot her. She was trespassing on private property at the time, and was in flight when the bullet hit her. She didn't see the shot fired. And if she had seen it, it'd be her word against his. No, if we're going to get Kozinsky, we'll have to get a witness. Or a confession. And the latter ain't bloody likely."

"Talbott must have been a witness."

"So he's going to admit chasing after Kozinsky when he's supposed to be confined to a wheelchair? You're out of your mind, Riordan. You know a lot better than that. I think Reiko's being shot has addled your brain. Come out of it."

He was right. I was out of my mind. I knew there was no case against Kozinsky, and that nothing in the world would get Talbott to testify. But what about Nick Costa? Was he a party to fraud? Or maybe the victim of a con? A smart lawyer with Costa's record of successes would never get himself involved with somebody like Talbott. Unless. . . .

Extortion. Blackmail. Threats of bodily harm. Somehow, I couldn't make anything fit. Talbott had only moved into the area six or eight months earlier. Kozinsky was an ox with a record of assault and battery but no major convictions. The only person I could get to who would know all the details was Nick Costa.

I said goodbye to Balestreri, adjuring him to leave no stone unturned in his investigation, and looked up the number of Costa's office in Monterey.

When I called, I was told by an officious female voice that Mr. Costa was in court, but that he would be in after two o'clock that afternoon. Would I care to make an appointment? "Sure," I said, "put me down for two-thirty. Pat Riordan. He knows who I am."

I drove slowly down into Monterey and climbed the steps to the little office on Alvarado Street that used to be over a bakery but is now atop an Italian restaurant and delicatessen which sends up an entirely new set of aromas. Reiko and I have been here about six years now, since we moved down from San Francisco. Without her, the place was like a tomb. Even the goddam computer didn't look so menacing. I flopped in my chair and sat forlornly contemplating my desk calendar which was totally blank. Without Reiko to keep track of things for me, I was lost.

There was a small noise beyond the partition. I got up and went to my door. Standing in the outer doorway was Cordelia Pompilio, the only member of the cast of *Waiting for the L-*

Train that I had not yet talked with. She was taller than I remembered, and older. But I had not forgotten that bright red hair.

"Mr. Riordan? Lieutenant Miller of the Carmel Police told me you might like to talk to me about Benjy's death. I happened to be in town today—my dentist is just up the street—so I thought I'd drop in. The Lieutenant told you, I suppose, that Benjy was my nephew."

"Yes, ma'am. Please sit down. It's not a very comfortable chair, but it's all I've got."

"I am Cordelia Pompilio. . . ."

"Yes, ma'am. I know. Named after the character in *King Lear*. Sally said that when she introduced us."

"Oh, have we met? You'll have to excuse me. My memory is so bad sometimes. But I don't know how I could have forgotten somebody like *you*." She was being coy. I am not prepossessing. I do not stick in peoples' minds for extended periods of time.

"I'm sorry about your nephew. Is it Miss, Mrs. or Ms. Pompilio?"

"Oh, it's Mrs. I'm not Italian, Mr. Riordan. My husband was a restaurateur on the Peninsula for many years. He passed away in '82. We had no children, more's the pity. As a matter of fact, the only child on my side of the family was Benjy. We were so proud of him."

I was not sure at the time if Cordelia was as terribly proud of Benjy as she professed, or if she was playing a role. The expressions, the inflections, were a little too studied.

"One thing has puzzled me, Mrs. Pompilio—"

"Please call me Cordelia. Everybody does."

"One thing has puzzled me, Cordelia. Why did you not tell anyone about your relationship with Benjy Noble until after his death?"

She registered sadness on cue. "My late husband never liked Benjy very much, Mr. Riordan. He had this terrible prejudice against homosexuals. Perverts, he called them. Well, I was never too comfortable with Benjy, either, but he was my own flesh and blood—my maiden name was Noble—and I just felt that he must do what he had to do. He wrote such wonderful plays." She registered something like awe.

"You claimed Benjy's body. I suppose he's to be shipped back to New York for burial."

"Oh, no. He left no special instructions. So I had the body cremated. And yesterday his ashes were scattered at sea. Of course, he probably would have preferred the *Atlantic* Ocean, but I doubt he'll know the difference."

Cordelia smiled a demure smile and shook her brick-red curls.

22
"We sent him to military school."

I STARED FOR a long moment at Cordelia Pompilio. The little smile remained on her face as her hands busied themselves plucking at her blouse and smoothing out her skirt.

Inspiration struck. "Do you know Alison Hargrove, Mrs. Pompilio?"

There was just the faintest flicker of her eyes, an almost imperceptible tightening along the jaw.

"Of course," she snapped. "Everyone knows Alison Hargrove, that pretentious old woman. Have you spoken to her? Has she told you anything about me?"

"I take it that there might be some bad blood between you and Miss Hargrove."

"She tells such awful lies, Mr. Riordan." The actress was beginning to take hold again. The face was controlled, the inflections theatrical. "I suppose she told you of her long and illustrious Broadway career. Well, I happen to know that she had walk-ons in three shows in 1949 and 1950. Then she met Lars Halvorsen and he humored her the rest of her life. Oh, I guess now she really believes what she tells people. But her theatrical career was confined for three decades to the Monterey Peninsula. I had more parts in New York than Alison ever dreamed of. Until, of course, Mr. Pompilio swept me off my feet and brought me to California. He was such a wonderful man, Mr. Riordan."

"But you must be much younger than Alison Hargrove."

I said the right thing. I often say the right thing. Cordelia did that cutesy little head toss again and smiled broadly, revealing expensive dentures, which, like reconstructed noses and bad toupees, are easy to identify.

"You are kind, Mr. Riordan. Alison is a few years my senior, but not as many as you might think."

"To get back to what I was thinking about, Cordelia, Miss Hargrove told me that she heard a strange sound down in the theater on the night Benjy Noble was killed, and then saw somebody running away down the hill. Do you think she really saw or heard anything, or could she have been imagining things? You know the lady. Is she . . . always in her best mental state?"

"You're asking me if I think Alison Hargrove is crazy? Of course not! She may be old, but she's sharp as a tack. Too sharp, sometimes. Whatever she may have told you or the police, whether it was the truth or something she made up, she told you for what she considered a good reason. No, the only thing she's fuzzy about these days is her theatrical career."

I wasn't sure how to take Cordelia Pompilio. With the fake red hair and the actressy ways, she made full acceptance of what she said a bit difficult. But I couldn't think of much more to ask her at that first meeting. Except one thing:

"Were you close to your nephew when he was younger, Cordelia?"

"I practically raised the boy. His mother ran off when he was nine, and his father—my only brother—died two years later of what I insisted at the time was a broken heart. Actually, it was cancer, but we don't like to talk about that."

"Benjy was an orphan? And you took him in."

"We were living in Salinas. Mr. Pompilio had three restaurants at the time, one in Salinas, others in Monterey and Pacific Grove. They were called Palermo I, II, and III. You must remember them."

"No, ma'am, I can't say I do."

"A shame, Mr. Riordan. Mr. Pompilio made the most wonderful veal piccata. And saltimbocca. And people would come for miles for his pasta, made fresh daily." She sounded like an ad in the phone book.

"So you raised Benjy Noble?"

"Well, I did and I didn't. Mr. Pompilio was not awfully fond of children, and he seemed to dislike Benjy right from the start. We sent him to military school. Back East someplace. Indiana, I think. Then he went to USC. Mr. Pompilio paid all the bills cheerfully enough. But he would leave the house whenever Benjy came to visit."

"I don't know if I asked this before, Cordelia, but I assume Mr. Pompilio is dead."

Business of the back of the hand pressed against the forehead. "Yes. And the pain of his loss has never abated."

Now, that sounded like a line from a play, but I wasn't going to pursue it any further. But one other thing did occur to me:

"How did Mr. Pompilio die, Cordelia? A long illness?"

"Oh, no. In the fire. In that awful fire that destroyed his Monterey restaurant. Everybody knows that. He had been working late, tallying up the day's receipts. It was before all those computerized cash registers. A fire started in the kitchen, and he was trapped in his office upstairs." She was obviously feeling "the pain of his loss" now, and tears were welling up in her eyes. The actress was being replaced by the woman.

I went to Cordelia and put my hand on her shoulder.

"I'm sorry. But I have to ask questions. You understand. Every little bit helps in this kind of investigation."

She regained her composure, and I escorted her to the door.

"One more question, Cordelia. I'm sorry, but I've got to ask. Was there any suspicion of arson in the fire?"

"Oh, there was no suspicion at all. It was arson. The firemen confirmed it the next day."

23

"I fell in love with her buns."

I HELPED CORDELIA POMPILIO out the door and down the steep stairs to Alvarado Street. She leaned heavily on my arm, and it was as if the weight of the memory of her husband's death was burdening her. She waved weakly as she walked across the street and disappeared in the walkway that leads up to Calle Principal. At that moment I had an uneasy feeling that there was something I had missed in my conversation with Cordelia. Or a question I should have asked.

When I got back up to the office, the phone was ringing insistently.

I scarcely had time to say hello, when an agitated Greg Farrell began yelling at me.

"Where's Reiko? I've been calling all over. She's not at her apartment, and she hasn't been in the office for a couple of days. Where is she, Pat? Is she sick or something?"

I didn't quite know how to tell him. So I decided just to lay it all out up front.

"She was shot, Greg. She was on a surveillance and a guy shot her. She's going to be OK. . . ."

110

"Shot! My God, is she dying? Where is she?"

"I was trying to tell you. She's going to be OK. She's up at Community Hospital, but she'll be going home in a couple of days. Her mother's down from San Jose, and she'll take care of Reiko until she's all recovered."

"You sonofabitch! You sent her on a job you should have done yourself. *You* got her shot."

"Get hold of yourself, Greg. She's my partner, remember? And she was on what was supposed to be a routine surveillance of an insurance claimant suspected to be malingering. Those people rarely shoot anybody. But the case appears to be turning into something else. I'm just as upset about it as you are."

He seemed to calm down a little. "Sorry, Pat. Where was she wounded? I mean, I took a few bullets in Viet Nam, and I can pretty well tell how bad it is."

I described the wound and the damage the doctor told me about.

"Ow, that hurts. And the nick in the bowel? They say how much of a nick?"

"I do not ask for clinical details. The doctor said everything was repaired. She seemed in reasonably good spirits when I visited her in the hospital this morning. You might run up there this afternoon, but I warn you, Mama-san is going to be there, and probably assorted other relatives."

"Has she got a phone? Can I call her?"

"I don't know, Greg. Call the goddam hospital and they'll give you all the scoop."

There was a pause at the other end.

"You know, Pat, I think I'm hooked on that lady. First time in a long time for me."

It was as close to a declaration of love as I have ever heard from Farrell. He has a favorite story about an incident that occurred on one of his tours in Viet Nam. The guys were all watching a movie in the balmy Southeast Asian out-of-doors, dodging fruit bats on the wing. And there was this scene with Hayley Mills, where she is taking a bath in a crude old-fashioned zinc bathtub. Somebody comes to the door and the camera is looking from behind Hayley as a man enters. She rises from the tub holding a towel in front of her, but, as Greg puts it, "She was naked in back, Riordan. I fell in love with her buns. I fell in love with Hayley Mills' ass." Which may account for the many bare-assed ladies Greg has painted over the years.

I don't altogether approve of his relationship with Reiko. Greg is nearly fifteen years older than she is, and I know him for what he is: an enormously talented artist who lives and does as he pleases. But I know Reiko pretty well, also, and I'm sure she can protect herself in the clinches.

"Call her, Greg. Hang up and call Reiko. I know she'll be happy to hear from you."

Which, I guess, he did.

I left my lonely office and wandered down Alvarado Street towards Fisherman's Wharf, the *old* wharf, once the genuine article, now a tourist trap. It was a little after noon, and I was due at Nick Costa's office at two-thirty. Lots of time to kill. Costa's office is in the 400 block on Pacific with a lot of other attorneys. Like many others, he maintains another office in Salinas, near the county courthouse. The Monterey County phone book's Yellow Pages 37 through 97 are devoted to attorneys, some of whom take two-color half-page and full-page ads extolling their own virtues. Of course, I do a lot of work for some of these guys. But there are others I wouldn't touch with the proverbial ten-foot pole.

I wandered out onto the Wharf in search of nothing, looking at the tourists in their colorful native costumes, marvelling at how so many of them had ugly legs that they insisted on showing. Mine ain't beautiful, but I keep my pants on in public. I slipped into one of the smaller restaurants that has counter service and ordered a calamari sandwich and a cup of coffee. The guy who had sat there ahead of me had left a *San Francisco Chronicle*. It's a paper I never see unless somebody else buys it. But it's got some features I like. I was browsing through the entertainment pages when my eye hit an article entitled "Who Killed Benjy Noble?" This being a subject of considerable interest to me, I took the time to read it all.

It seems the writer had some theories about Noble's murder. "Benjy Noble," he wrote, "was one of the twentieth century's great playwrights. He won many honors. He had many enemies. What jealous rival could have plunged the fatal dagger into Noble's throat and left his bleeding body on a crude stage in Carmel?"

Well, firstly, it wasn't a dagger. Secondly, the stage wasn't crude. Thirdly, Benjy wasn't all that great. I read the piece through to the end with a broad smile on my face. The writer had leaped to all sorts of improbable conclusions. He had pursued the notion that the dastardly deed was done by a professional rival in a fit of jealousy. Although who Benjy Noble's "professional rival" might have been was certainly unclear. It was a cut above the kind of story you might find in one of those supermarket tabloids. But just as full of holes.

At twenty after two, I headed uptown toward Pacific Street and the offices of Nick Costa. I walked in the door at precisely two-thirty. The properly officious receptionist eyed me suspiciously. I think I looked like a rapist or a pederast to her.

"May I help you?" Icicles formed on her tones.

"Have an appointment with Mr. Costa. Pat Riordan."

She looked disgusted. "Oh, yes, the private investigator. Sit down."

"Any particular place?"

"Seat yourself where you please, Mr. Riordan. I'll see if Mr. Costa is in."

I was spending too much time in offices waiting for important people.

"I have an appointment with Mr. Costa. If I'm not mistaken, you made it for me. Mr. Costa has *got* to be in."

The officious lady stood up abruptly. "Your manners are not very good, are they, Mr. Riordan. I'll see if Mr. Costa can see you."

I was about to say the sonofabitch had better see me when she slipped through the door of the great man's private office.

In a couple of minutes, she returned. "Mr. Costa will see you now, Mr. Riordan. Please keep in mind that he is a very busy man and keep your visit short. Thank you."

What a pain in the ass.

I went through the door. Costa was sitting at his desk. His face was flushed and he was sweating profusely. He was fumbling with an unlit cigar.

"Take a seat, Riordan," he said. "Want a drink?"

"I do not drink alcohol, Nick. It's a fetish. Don't smoke either."

"Don't worry. I don't intend to light this thing. Doctor took me off them five years ago. Now I just use the cigar as a prop. You know, like George Burns or Groucho Marx." He smiled weakly. I refrained from telling him that both Burns and Marx actually smoked their cigars.

Costa leaned forward with his hands clasped together on his desk, the cigar jutting out from between his fingers.

"I know why you're here, Riordan. You're going to ask me why that girl got shot, aren't you?"

24
"I have this problem."

I HAVE GOT TO admit that he was direct. I hadn't really expected Costa to lay it on the line like that. Something was making him sweat. The cigar in his hand was showing wet spots. His shirt was plastered to his body under a totally unnecessary tropical-weight jacket that looked like he had slept in it. He even *smelled* bad.

"As a matter of fact, that's not what I was going to ask you, counselor. I know why she was shot. She had just witnessed the fact that Charlie Talbott isn't paralyzed. That big hireling of yours instinctively decided to kill her. What I came here to ask is why you have such a worthless bastard on your payroll."

"He's not on my payroll, Riordan. You might say I'm on his. Oh, it goes back a long way. Kozinsky had something on me. In the beginning, I just played along with him. Whenever he got in trouble, I'd get Howard Gravesend to defend him. God help me, I even fixed a juror in one of the cases. And he'd leave me alone for a few months. Then there'd be something else. This latest thing was the Talbott case. He had met

Talbott at a bar up in Moss Landing. They both had a lot to drink, and Talbott told him how easy it was to fake an injury and collect a lot of money from insurance companies. He had done it a couple of times, and hadn't had to work a lick for six or seven years. So they planned another scam together.

"It was pretty clever, how they did it. They got hold of some information about interstate truckers. Then they chose a likely run and went up along Highway One north of Castroville and parked Talbott's car on a side road where it couldn't be seen. This was at night, you understand, and it took a lot of precision. Talbott allowed Kozinsky to beat him up to produce convincing injuries. It must have been painful. That guy is a brute. But the cuts and bruises were necessary.

"It seems that Talbott had this old spinal injury that had healed long ago. But he had been told that it could give him trouble in the future. This knowledge was what he had depended on in his two previous scams. And he was confident he could get away with it again.

"They had it timed to the minute. When the big rig came down the pike, they pushed Talbott's car out of the side road right in front of it. The truck driver hit the brakes, but he couldn't avoid the collision. Then, in the confusion, Talbott ran to a ditch on the other side of the road and lay down. That was about it. The paramedics treated him for cuts and bruises. He insisted that his lower body was numb. Couple of doctors examined him and said the paralysis could be the result of new trauma on the old injury. Voilà, personal injury case."

"Which is where you got into the case." I was impressed. Never in all my dealings with lawyers have I heard such a straightforward presentation. Maybe that's why I never took the bar exam a second or third or fourth time. Despite my legal education, I could never have argued for the acquittal of somebody I knew to be guilty of a felony. I would have had a hard time pushing contingency cases around until I could get a bigger percentage. And here before me was a prominent Monterey County attorney pouring out enough guilt to convict himself.

"It's not as simple as that," he said. "I knew all about the thing as it was being planned. It's what I told you, Riordan. That gorilla had something on me and I couldn't cut him loose."

"What did he have on you?"

The face sagged. Costa was fleshy around the jowls anyhow, and his head seemed to be melting into his collar. The cigar in his hand snapped in two.

"I have this problem. It . . . involves young children. It's . . . something I can't help. Kozinsky has pictures of me. It'll all come out now. I'm finished. I thought I could handle it, but . . . Well, the bastard might have killed that girl. I've done some pretty shady things, Riordan. But not murder . . . nor violence of any kind."

"What about your family, Nick. You going to throw them to the dogs?"

"I have no family. No wife or kids . . . for obvious reasons."

"Then, what are you going to do? Throw yourself on the mercy of the court? Testify against Talbott and Kozinsky?"

"That's about it. I'm finished. I'm the only one who'll suffer. Except her," he said, indicating the outer office. "Except Florence. I don't know what she'll do. Nobody in Monterey will hire her. She's a nasty bitch . . . but efficient."

I asked to use the telephone and relayed to Tony Balestreri the information I had just received. "Where are these guys now," he asked. I turned to Costa.

"Do you know where Talbott and Kozinsky are right now?"

"Yeah, they're at Talbott's place in New Monterey. I sent 'em there after the shooting with my kindest advice to stay put. Tell your friend to be careful, though. The big guy is a mean one. He'll shoot it out."

"I'm on my way," said Balestreri when I told him where to go. "We'll have this thing wrapped up in a half hour."

"Don't get hurt, Tony," I said, and hung up.

Costa seemed a little calmer than he had been when I arrived. His color was better, and he was lighting one of halves of his busted cigar. "So who gives a damn, now? What have I got to live for? I'll do some time. And then maybe somebody will hire me to do what you do. Couldn't be that hard."

"I wish I could feel sorry for you, Nick. Maybe I could sympathize about your being blackmailed into this mess. But I don't think I could ever forgive or understand a grown man who gets his jollies with innocent kids. Or do you guys just think of yourselves as another voting minority?"

I left Costa's office, blowing a kiss to Florence on my way out. I would like to have heard a shot from the inner sanctum as I left, but you just can't count on some guys to do the right thing at the right time. Costa didn't disappoint me altogether, though. After I left his office, he must have done some very serious thinking.

The bright sunlight and cool breeze had a kind of cleansing effect on me as I walked down Franklin a couple of blocks to Alvarado. Back in my office, I called Braverman at the insurance company and told' him it was all over. He seemed happy, but he didn't offer to take me to dinner.

"I'll put a check in the mail in the morning, Pat. Keep in touch."

Without Reiko, the mail had stacked up for a couple of days. Not that any of it is all that important. Advertising throwaways, offers to lend me money. Somehow these financial outfits have me pegged as a property owner and they offer me all kinds of loans. Once a week, like clock work, some mysterious bank from someplace I've never heard of, sends me an application for a credit card. And there are always the bills.

I was sitting at my desk, wondering which bills to pay and which to drop in my desk drawer, when Reiko's Uncle Shiro stuck his head in. Shiro, who was born in Fresno, raised in Japan to high school age, but returned to Los Angeles for his secondary education, speaks English with a flair that is all his own.

"So how do you feel, hot shot? You happy now you got that little girl in the hospital. You some kind of *schmeckel*, you know that? The rent's due tomorrow."

"Shiro, I know you won't believe me, but I didn't mean to

send Reiko out to be shot. She wanted to work on this case. She had to follow those guys. What can I say after I say I'm sorry."

"Don't give me song lyrics, hot shot. Just pay the rent." And he disappeared.

On my way into Carmel that evening I was aware of heavier traffic than usual and congestion downtown that was not characteristic of that time of day. Then I heard the bagpipes and it dawned on me that the weekend of the Scottish Games was upon us. I parked in my drive and walked down the hill to watch the parade.

It may be one of the shortest parades known to civilized man. From Devendorf Park down Ocean to Monte Verde, back up Ocean to San Carlos, down San Carlos to the Red Lion Tavern. There's a bagpipe band, and some husky characters carrying the caber, a wooden pole that muscular Scots heave in competition.

It was colorful. A relief from an exhausting day. There's something about bagpipes. The Irish use bagpipes, too, although nobody thinks much about that. But on that special summer evening, the bagpipe band was skirling out traditional Scottish melodies. All except a single piper bringing up to the rear of the entire column, bravely playing snatches from Beethoven's Ninth.

I watched the parade go by on San Carlos, and trudged wearily over to the Bully III on Dolores for something to eat.

Later, Balestreri called me at the house. "We got 'em, soldier. Kozinsky and Talbott. The big guy fired a few shots, but we had 'em bottled up. Talbott's wife was there, too. They're all in the can. Talbott was running like crazy. We've got confessions from the three of 'em. But, there's something else. . . ."

"Don't keep me in suspense, Tony. I don't need any more aggravation after this day."

"Your buddy Costa. They found him floating under Wharf #2. He's out of it, Pat."

No surprise.

"We're better off, Sergeant. We're better off."

25
"*I am used to taking difficult objectives, Pat.*"

W<small>HERE DO</small> I find the sonofabitch?"

I was standing in my shorts before an open door through which cold damp air was pouring. Moments before I had run down the narrow stairs from the bedroom in answer to a loud knocking and shouting.

Greg Farrell was standing on the doorstep in full combat uniform, camouflage fatigues, military beret, and boots. Strapped at his side was a wicked looking forty-five automatic.

"That depends on who you're looking for, Greg," I said sweetly. "There are considerably more sons of bitches in this world than there are bitches, just as there are many more horses' asses than there are horses. Which sonofabitch do you seek?"

He pushed me firmly in the chest and I backed into the room.

"Get in there. I don't want you catching cold. You know

goddam well who I'm looking for. The filthy bastard who shot Reiko."

"I know how you must feel, but you're a few hours too late. Tony Balestreri in cooperation with the Monterey Police took Kosinsky, Talbott, and Mrs. Talbott into custody late yesterday afternoon. If you wish to visit any one of them, I could get you into the county jail. But you'd have to check the gun."

Greg seemed terribly disappointed. He is usually a sweet-natured sort of person. I think he had more than enough experience with guns and bloodshed in Viet Nam, just as I did in Korea. But the wounding of Reiko had got his old combat spirit up. He would have been overjoyed if he had been able to participate in the capture of Kosinsky and Talbott. Hearing that the party was over, he was crestfallen.

"What'll they get, Pat? Gas chamber's out, huh?"

"There's no murder involved. And in California the death penalty can be invoked only under certain circumstances. They'll get a lot of time for the fraud, and the two men will be charged with ADW. That's about the size of it. Howard Gravesend isn't around any more to defend."

"What about that sleazy lawyer, that Costa? He sure as hell will be charged, too, won't he?"

"Too late for that, too, Greg. They found him floating under Wharf #2 last night. Coroner's preliminary says suicide. The guy was a child molester. Kosinsky had the evidence. That's how they got hooked up."

Greg sat down heavily on my couch. "I would have blasted all three of the men, and maybe even the woman if I had the chance. I was that mad, Pat. Then I would be in the tank, with a lot of counts of homicide. I'm still mad, but I'm beginning to feel relieved that I didn't have the opportunity to go berserk." He looked up at me with an expression I had never seen before on his bearded face. "I must be in love. Now, ain't that a gas."

"It's not fatal. But you have bought yourself a lot of ready-made obstacles. Reiko's pretty old-fashioned, and she thinks about marriage. I do not try to deceive myself into thinking she's a virgin. But I suspect that she wouldn't enter into any long-term relationship without some sort of ceremony, preferably Buddhist. And you, my friend, are not known for your susceptibility to marriage. So be advised. Besides, you'd have a hell of a time getting past Mama-san."

He became the soldier again. "I am used to taking difficult objectives, Pat. Why, they used to say, 'After companies and battalions have failed, just send in Farrell.' Or words to that effect."

"That is probably bullshit, and I choose to ignore it. Reiko isn't a hill or a village. You don't just 'take' her. But I can see that I am talking to a brick wall. Let me get dressed and I'll treat you down at the Bagel Bakery."

I managed to get him to leave the gun in the car when we went into the bagel shop. When we had finished several cups of coffee and a bagel-and-a-half with cream cheese each, I drove him back up to the house and put him in his black pickup.

"Do you think it's too early to go to the hospital? I ought to go see her, I think."

"Go on over. If you can't get into her room, wait around until you can. Just stay out of trouble. Don't shoot up the place."

Off he drove with the roar of a bad muffler into the lifting fog.

I shaved and showered and drove over the hill to Monterey. One burden was off my back. Now the main thing I had to apply myself to was the murder of Benjy Noble. I began reviewing in my mind the interviews I had had with various people connected with the case. Nothing I could remember really helped me decide where to turn next.

The dilemma was solved at the office. On my phone answering device was a message from Charles Cartwright, the New York psychiatrist who had treated Noble. He had called from a San Francisco hotel, and his voice was urgent. I called him back right away.

"Dr. Cartwright. This is Pat Riordan in Monterey. You wanted to talk to me?"

"Riordan? Oh, yes, you're the investigator Hal Denby hired to look into Benjy Noble's murder. Lieutenant Miller of the Carmel Police said you'd like to talk to me."

"You bet, Doctor. How do we do this? It'll take some time and I don't want to run up the phone bill. Shall I come up there."

"That won't be necessary. I'm checking out in an hour, and I'm planning to rent a car and drive down to Monterey. I've arranged to meet Pam Hudson there. I understand you've already talked to her. I'll be going into the Marriott. How long should it take me to get there?"

"Let's see, it's a little after nine. If you leave about ten, you should be here by noon or so. Depending on how fast you drive. Have you driven in California before?"

"No. I assume the speed limit is the same as in the rest of the country. Fifty-five?"

"For the uninitiated, yes. But folks will pass you going seventy and eighty. If you stick to the double nickel, you'll have some trucker rolling over you. Just use your own judgment and stay out of the fast lane."

"I'll call when I get in. I'm anxious to talk to you, Riordan. Benjy Noble was a complicated case. He had this obsession with having killed somebody. And I'm sure he couldn't have harmed a fly."

26

"We knew about the letters, Mr. Riordan."

W HEN I KNOCKED at his suite later that afternoon, Dr. Charles Cartwright opened the door so quickly he must have heard my footsteps.

"Mr. Riordan? Come in."

If I had seen him first on the street, I would never have taken the man for an expensive New York psychiatrist. Cartwright was balding and overweight. His shirt had a couple of days wear on it and was pulling out of his baggy trousers. He had not shaved that morning, and the fringe of hair around his oversized head was greasy and uncombed. His eyes were a few millimeters too close together, and his nostrils sprouted twin tufts of gray hair. He smiled automatically at me, displaying very large but perfectly even teeth. If I had been a patient meeting a doctor for the first time—especially a patient whose neuroses needed adjustment—I might have turned and fled.

Over Cartwright's shoulder I could see Pam Hudson sitting primly on a couch at one end of the room. The doctor had not stinted on his accommodations. It wasn't the presidential suite, but it was pretty fair digs, probably developing a tab on the order of $200 a day. Not a hell of a lot by New York standards, but jazzy for Monterey.

I nodded to Dr. Hudson and sat down on the couch beside her. "How are you? Still hot in San Jose?"

"Yes, rather, Mr. Riordan. Although it has cooled off since you visited me." She seemed pretty uncomfortable.

Cartwright stood before us in a stance not unlike that of a plate umpire, legs planted, hands behind back, stooping forward. "I have been comparing notes with Dr. Hudson. I'm pleased to find that her opinion of the case agrees with mine in nearly all details. Of course, she has much nicer legs." The toothy smile again which suddenly seemed repulsive to me. However, I couldn't help glancing at Pam Hudson's legs. She, on the other hand, instinctively tugged at her skirt and blushed.

The New York specialist began to pace. "Dr. Hudson has told me that even in the short time she had with Benjy Noble she sensed some deep underlying disturbance that he had repressed for perhaps a considerable length of time. I treated the man for three years, long after I first met him as a backer of his early plays. Benjy came to me as a friend soon after he had his first success. He was disturbed and unhappy, even though he was for the first time in his career experiencing recognition and financial independence. All during the time he was writing what was to become his Pulitzer Prize and Tony Award-winning play, he seemed extraordinarily depressed.

"I am used to dealing with theater people. Some have terrible problems with success. Once achieved, it must be sustained. And that's what scares the hell out of a lot of actors, directors, and playwrights. They ask themselves if they can do it again. They live in mortal dread that what has been found may be lost again overnight. There are a lot of crazy people in the theater.

"But I thought I knew Benjy Noble well enough to support him and allay his fears. However, I found in our earliest sessions as doctor and patient that although he was as insecure as any writer who has had one success and wonders whether he can do it again, there was something much deeper that was dragging Benjy down. And more than once he said to me what he said most recently to Dr. Hudson: 'I killed him, I killed him.' Then he would fall silent and no amount of cajoling could get him to talk again during a session.

"I tried everything I knew. Regression under hypnotism was a failure. Some people cannot be hypnotized, you know. I was on the verge of using chemicals to search his memory, but it was about that time that he finished *Memories of Jackson,* and he went into a period of excited anticipation that seemed to erase his depression entirely. A couple of months later, the play was produced with great success. Then came the awards. Benjy was on top of the world. For a little while. Then the inevitable let-down. Could he do it again?

"He went to work on the next play—the one he came here for, *Waiting for the L-Train*—and seemed to be sliding again into depression. It appeared to me that it worsened when he— I think, somewhat reluctantly—agreed at Hal Denby's insistence to premiere the show in Carmel. Benjy had confided in me that he had never particularly liked Denby, despite the fact that Hal had been an investor in some of his early losing efforts. Hal had not been a very good loser in those early days. Like many wealthy men, he hates to see an investment go sour. But he was convinced of Benjy's talent. I think Hal has been bitter for not having been invited to put some of his dollars in *Memories of Jackson,* but I suspect he would have passed, anyhow."

Dr. Cartwright ceased his pacing, which was making me nervous. It was sort of like sitting at mid-court during a tennis match and watching the ball go back and forth, back and forth. He flopped down in a large easy chair opposite Pam Hudson and me, and clasped his hands across his well-nourished middle.

"I do not think—and Dr. Hudson agrees with me—that Benjy Noble could have killed somebody. I don't think he was suffering from a severe psychosis. He was an imaginative soul, as a playwright must be. I have concluded that Benjy's admission of 'killing' a person, a 'him', was probably rooted in his having written something so closely related to his own life, that he had convinced himself that he had truly done something that he had only imagined. I think Dr. Hudson will concur."

I stretched and covered a yawn. "I'm sorry. Didn't get my sleep out, I guess. This has been terribly interesting, Doctor. But not very helpful. What I'm looking for is a motive for murder. None of what you've told me has helped me understand why anybody would lure Benjy Noble to the Forest Theater in the middle of the night and kill him." I turned to Pam Hudson. "What do you think."

She turned prim on me. "Mr. Riordan, in psychiatry we can only draw certain conclusions from the facts as presented by the patient. We are trained at eliciting information by careful questioning. Analysis can only go so far. . . ."

I stood up. "Thanks a lot, folks. Now I know what I knew all along. Benjy was disturbed. A couple of times he confessed to murder during analysis. Two psychiatrists say it was imaginary. Back to the old drawing board." I started for the door, but something I had almost forgotten about stopped me.

"Did Benjy ever mention some letters he got this past spring—to either one of you? Letters from somebody who claimed that he had stolen the idea for *Waiting for the L-Train*. Signed by a fellow named Lindemann."

The two doctors exchanged glances. Each was waiting for the other to respond. Finally, Cartwright cleared his throat and spoke:

"We knew about the letters, Mr. Riordan. Just another manifestation of some sort of deep-rooted guilt. Benjy brought the first one to me during a session in April. He was very agitated. I looked at the letter. It was mainly gibberish interlarded with accusations of plagiarism. But I recognized the peculiarities of the typewriter. The letters had been turned out on Benjy's old machine. He wrote them himself."

27
"He really was a nice man."

I MADE A low bow to the psychiatrists and departed. When I pressed into the crowded elevator, I was lost in my thoughts until I heard a slightly irritated female voice speaking my name.

"That was no way to treat a lady."

I turned and looked upon Christy Burgess, the fabulous ingénue, whose streaky blonde hair was just under my nose and whose breasts were pressed against me. Elevators have a way of creating intimate encounters. She looked up at me with an expression of mock anger, and pressed just a little closer.

"Hello, Christy. Visiting somebody?"

"I'm not sure what you mean, but I think it's dirty. Actually, I was delivering a gown to a client who comes down from San Francisco just to shop in our store. What are *you* doing in a hotel at this time of day?"

"Taking you to lunch. Unless you've eaten."

"As a matter of fact I haven't. And you really owe me." She squirmed a little and I felt the blood rushing to areas that might embarrass me.

In the lobby I led Christy to the coffee shop. She sniffed. "You could do better than this. I know a couple of places. . . ."

I stopped her. "Christy, I promise I'll take you to a fancy lunch, or even dinner, sometime in the not too distant future. However, I've got some things to do this afternoon and we'll have to grab a quick bite. How's this?" I pointed to a table on the edge of the crowded restaurant.

"You missed a wonderful meal the other day, Pat. I love the food at Guglielmo's and the waiters make me feel so good. You really didn't leave enough money, though. I had to come up with the tip myself." She pouted a practiced pout. "But you shouldn't have left me like that. Without any explanation at all."

I told her all about Reiko and what had happened. It didn't seem to affect her much.

"And is your friend going to be all right? I hope so. That sort of thing shouldn't happen to a woman, should it? I mean, really. I *know* about the feminist movement, but women should stay . . . well, real feminine, don't you think? Being shot . . . ugh. Gives me the shivers."

"Christy, I have it on good authority that very often extremely feminine women get shot. Husbands do it, or boy friends. Reiko was simply shot in the line of duty. She was doing her job."

"Well, I still don't believe in it." She turned up a pretty little nose.

I changed the subject. "Christy, I'm getting a sort of composite picture of Benjy Noble. Everybody who had any contact with him has given me a little something. But not really enough. Aside from the fact that I know you were on the make for him until you found out he was gay—"

"Who told you that?" She bristled.

"Doesn't matter. It's true, isn't it?"

She frowned a small frown, something she did infrequently to avoid cultivating creases between her brows. "I will do anything necessary to help my career. Actually, I found Benjy quite attractive. But he made it a point early in our relation-

ship that he . . . uh . . . marched to a different drummer. He
didn't seem swishy, you know what I mean. He talked real
normal."

"Many do, my child, many do. But I'm looking for some
other knowledge about Benjy Noble. Did he ever confide in
you about something else? Anything else?"

She thought about it. "He did tell me Cordelia was his
aunt. Said not to tell anybody. But then I think he told everybody. In the cast, that is."

"Is that it?"

"I guess. He really was a nice man."

The waitress was upon us. Christy ordered some sort of
exotic salad and I asked for a reuben sandwich and a cup of
coffee. She chattered gaily between bites when the food
arrived, and I was bored silly. Her tasty little body was safe
from me. You know, I never thought I'd say that.

I put Christy on the bus for Carmel after lunch, making
the excuse that I would have driven her but I had an important meeting to attend. She kissed me lightly on the cheek
when she left, and waved goodbye from the bus window.

There was no way I wanted to go back to my empty office.
After my earlier session with Benjy's guilt, I didn't want to
have to face my own. All it took was Reiko's vacant chair and
the dead green screen on her computer.

I called Sally Morse's office. "You busy?" I asked.

"Not really. Just putting together a group presentation for
some senior citizens organization. They think they want to go
to Alaska."

"Is it cold in the summer? "

"If you go far enough, it's plenty cold. But you didn't call
for a geography lesson. What's up?"

"I'm trying to get a complete picture of Benjy Noble. So
far, I've got fragments. Can you add anything?"

"So, what do you know?"

"He was a successful playwright. Very successful. He was
orphaned at an early age and more or less raised by Cordelia
and her husband. He was homosexual and a manic-depres-

sive. He had this terrible guilt about something. There were some threatening letters that turned out to have been written by Benjy to himself under the name of Lindemann. Everybody claims to have loved the man like a son or a brother or some other close relative. So far, there is not a goddam thing to suggest why somebody might have killed him. Any idea? *Any idea?*"

"You know more than I do, Pat. Afraid I can't help."

"Who could, Sal? Suggestions?"

"You might try Maria Theresa O'Higgins. She's known him longer than anybody. She directed most of his better known plays."

"Great. Where do I find her?"

"She rented a little house down on Lincoln, between Eleventh and Twelfth. She wanted quiet and peace, she said. I think she wanted a place to drag her victims to after she stung 'em. Go at your own risk." She gave me a Carmel phone number to call.

"Bless you. This might throw a lot of light on something or other. How about dinner this evening?"

"You sure you're still hungry after lunching with that hot little cutie?"

"How'd you know about that?"

"I'm a travel agent, Patrick. My spies are everywhere. I will assume that you were pumping Christy for information. Or have you been pumping Christy?"

"I'm hurt. If you know me as well as you say you do, you know damn well I couldn't be seduced by that little air-head." I crossed my fingers just slightly.

"OK. I'll accept that for the moment. But I'd rather not hear about it again."

Sally's possessiveness gave me a real warm feeling. I've suggested marriage to her, believe it or not, on a number of occasions. But she has resisted, claiming that she valued her independence too much. But, maybe sometime. . . .

"Thank you, kindly, ma'am. I will look up Madame O'Higgins and see what she has to say."

"One other thing, Pat. See if she can tell you why Benjy wanted to be anonymous to the public. Why he wanted to use the pseudonym, Anna Leiser?"

28
"Please call me Maria."

ANNA LEISER. Analyzer. I hadn't thought of that for a long time. The connection with Pam Hudson and Charles Cartwright was too goddam obvious. Was Benjy so trapped in his analysis that he had become an "analyzer"? I remembered what Hudson had said at our meeting in San Jose. To become an analyst, you have to be analyzed by an analyst who, in turn, has been analyzed, and so on, *ad infinitum*. Benjy, having been analyzed by a couple of analysts, declared himself an "analyzer."

The whole thing was beginning to sound pretty looney. Benjy Noble was a looney. A brilliant looney, but nevertheless certifiable. Some day I will have to see his Pulitzer Prize play. I understand it is now circulating among the more sincere little-theater groups.

I sighed and picked up the phone again to call Maria Theresa O'Higgins. After about eight rings, just as I was about to hang up, there came a voice from another galaxy: "*This* is O'Higgins, hello there."

"This is Patrick Riordan, Ms. O'Higgins. We met at the

Forest Theater. At the first rehearsal. I was the guy who knew Sally. Remember?"

"Riordan. Yes, of course. A noble Irish name like mine. Our ancestors were kings, Riordan, did you know that? While the English were living in caves and painting themselves blue, our ancestors were kings."

I had heard that somewhere. Maria Theresa had appropriated it for her own.

Modestly, I recited my own lineage: "My great-grandfather was a potato farmer, Ms. O'Higgins, who came over here when the crop went sour in the 1850s. Well, maybe *his* ancestors were kings. I know many of 'em died in combat, but usually with fists and shillelaghs or bogwood cudgels. Be that as it may, I think you know that I'm investigating Benjy Noble's murder. Would it be possible for us to get together and talk about it? I understand you're possibly Benjy's oldest friend."

"Oldest *female* friend. Yes, I think so. What is it you want to talk about?"

"My composite picture of the man is pretty fuzzy. I am trying to figure out some sort of real motive for the killing. And, despite the information poured into my ears by his analysts and a few associates, I've come up empty. Can you think of any reason somebody might kill Benjy? Or anybody who hated him enough to kill him?"

"I must think, Riordan. Come to my house. It's on the east side of Lincoln between Eleventh and Twelfth. It is called Scrub Oak or Fumed Oak or something to that effect."

I've got to explain to the newcomers that Carmel has no house numbers and no mail delivery. You've got to have a quick, accurate description of your dwelling and its location to explain where you live. And you have to have a post office box to get your mail.

"I'll be there in about a half hour." I hung up the phone with the feeling that I'd find Maria Theresa in a darkened room dealing tarot cards. Or the back yard piled with the corpses of some of the town's younger studs.

True to my word, I pulled up in front of the house on Lincoln Street thirty-five minutes later. It was one of those little places of indeterminate age, remodeled four or five times. It sat on the back of the tight Carmel lot, up a long flight of precarious wooden stairs. I knocked on the top half of the Dutch door.

"Come. It's not locked."

I opened the door into a tiny living room dominated by a huge fireplace in which there glowed one of those composition logs you buy in the supermarket. Granted, although it was, for August, a coolish day, it was sure as hell not coolish enough for a fire.

"I love a fire, don't you?" said Maria Theresa O'Higgins. "It's so romantic." She was draped on a loveseat, dressed in the same black outfit she wore when we first met at the Forest Theater. The curtains were drawn and no lights were on. I looked around for the tarot cards.

"It's a wee bit hot for me, Ms. O'Higgins."

"Feel free to disrobe to whatever extent pleases you, Mr. Riordan. We easterners are not used to the nip in the air that seems to give you California coast people rosy cheeks. Your cheeks *are* rosy, aren't they, Mr. Riordan?"

It had been a long time since a woman had patently tried to seduce me, and now it had happened twice in the same day. Look here, I am a man of average height, with thinning hair and a thickening waist. I admit to being in some stage of middle-age, perhaps *advanced*. So the fact that two females were after my body within a couple of hours was causing me some confusion. I took a couple of deep breaths and told myself that the little cutie was just a tease, but this one was a barracuda.

"Ms. O'Higgins. . . ."

"Please call me Maria." She pronounced it *Muh-rye-uh*. "Nobody else does. They insist on making it Latin. But I like it the other way. You know, 'They call the wind Muh-rye-uh'." She sang the line in a very loud Ethel Merman voice. "Actually, it was Miriam. I'm Jewish. O'Higgins was a

drunken bum who thought he was a leading man. We were
divorced eons ago. But I do love his royal Irish name, don't
you?"

"'Tis indeed a marvelous name, macushlah." I was beginning to fall into the spirit of the bizarre situation. I didn't
know what the hell "macushlah" meant, but then neither did
she.

"Would you like a drink, Riordan? No? Well, I think I'll
have one." She got up slowly and walked a little unsteadily to
a small table and poured herself about three inches of straight
Scotch into a tall glass. She drained an inch of the stuff and
found her way back to the loveseat. "Why aren't you sitting
down?" she asked.

"I am now," I said, looking for a chair in the dim room.

"You have questions? Ask away."

The warmth of the fire and the heavy scent of musk drift-
ing from Maria Theresa was making me a little giddy. But I
charged ahead.

"Muh-rye-uh, why do you think anybody would kill
Benjy? Did anybody in New York have it in for him. Enough
to come out here and beat him to death?"

She took another sip of Scotch. When she spoke, her words
were beginning to slur and run together. The whiskey was not
her first libation of the day.

"I directed all but one of Benjy's plays. I am a very good
director. Oh, I know these *amateurs* don't think much of me.
But I don't think much of *them,* either. Benjy was merely fumbling and thrashing at the start. But I could see there was a
great talent there, so I stuck with him through all the flops.
And voilà, one day there was success. The Pulitzer Prize play
was not the first commercial success, you understand. He had
five plays that made it at the box office, five in a row. Then
the big one. All the prizes."

She looked into her glass as if to be sure there was booze
in it, and took another sip.

"O'Riordan, you'd think a man would be happy with all
that success, wouldn't you? Benjy never was. Oh, he had

moments of elation when the reviews came in, but he was never happy. Not one day was he happy. But he wrote like a madman, from morning until night, play after play. Some of 'em he just tore up. Others made it to the stage. And when they made it, they were *good.* God, were they good."

"It's just plain Riordan, ma'am. The O probably got knocked off at Ellis Island. You know some of those immigration guys couldn't spell. Neither could my great-grandfather. Let me ask you something specific. Hal Denby found this batch of threatening letters that Benjy's shrink says he wrote to himself. The were signed 'Paul Lindemann.' Does that name mean anything to you."

She looked up in surprise, her face twisted in something like a sneer. "Hell yes it does. And it should to Denby, too. It was the name of the lead character in Benjy's first play—the one Hal invested in that was such an awful flop—'Paul Lindemann.' Sure, I remember. That's why the play failed. All the critics said the same thing. Too down-beat, they said. Depressing. What they objected to, you know, was that 'Paul Lindemann' commits suicide in view of the audience, just as the curtain goes down."

29
"I am in a quandary, Reiko."

PAUL LINDEMANN. A creature of Benjy Noble's imagination who commits suicide on stage and writes threatening letters to Benjy accusing him of plagiarism. Except that Benjy wrote the letters to himself. And Benjy kept telling his shrinks that he had killed somebody.

I suppose it's logical—if there is any logic to be found in this mess—to assume that Benjy's confession of murder could be interpreted to mean that he had killed off Paul Lindemann in his first play by having the character commit suicide. *Or* that he felt that he had killed his own *play* by having his protagonist commit suicide. Or, with the privilege of the playwright, he was just playing God.

Maria Theresa had closed her eyes and was snoring loudly. I gently removed the glass from her limp fingers, grabbed her by the heels of her high black boots, and stretched her out on the couch. "Nighty-night," I said, and tiptoed out of the room.

The cool, bright air revived me as I came out of the warm, dark house into the world again. I had not learned a hell of a lot from Madame O'Higgins. It would have been futile to ask her about Anna Leiser. She probably thought it was Benjy's idea of a joke. And I suspect she didn't think it was very funny.

If I had only got to meet Benjy Noble, talk to him, get an idea of what kind of person he was. I really didn't know what he looked like. Hadn't even seen a picture of him.

It was late in the August afternoon, so I stopped at home. No point in going to the office. I was planning to pick up Sally at her Carmel office at five-thirty. A shower and a dash of cologne might make me more appealing. Or, at least, cleaner and smellier.

My house was built in 1928, and no amount of remodeling has ever quite corrected a flaw in the single bathroom. When I take a shower, part of the water from the shower nozzle goes out the bathroom window. No matter how I try to twist it, the stream either soaks the john seat, or goes out the window. If I forget to open the window, it all bounces back and I have a quarter of an inch of water on the bathroom floor when I'm finished, just beginning to seep through to the kitchen below unless I dash around naked and mop up the water with all the towels I own. This ritual has never been witnessed by another soul, thank God. And I seldom forget the window nowadays.

I didn't forget it this time. Toweling off and pulling on a clean pair of shorts, I picked up the phone, punched out the number of Community Hospital, and asked for Reiko's room.

"Hello," came a small voice.

"Reiko? This is Pat. You sound so weak. Are you all right?"

"Oh, yes," she said in a hoarse whisper, "it's just that Mama and Uncle Shiro are having this loud argument about Greg. I think Shiro wants to put out a hit on Greg, but Mama thinks it should be kept in the family. He was here when they arrived and, well, they caught him kissing me."

"What do you mean Mama wants to keep it in the family?" It sounded ominous to me.

"Well, she wants my cousin Otis Nakamura to beat Greg up. Otis runs a karate school, you know."

"So what are you doing about this? Are you going to let Farrell get hit, or will you suggest *hara kiri*?"

"Don't worry, it'll all blow over. I'll talk to them when they run out of steam. They do this all the time whenever I seem interested in somebody, whether he's Japanese or not. But I have to talk to them separately and tell each of them that the other is dead wrong. That always seems to satisfy them."

Then I asked what I wanted to ask in the first place. "How are you physically? I mean, how's the wound."

"It hurts now and then. But the doctors say it's healing nicely. I should be out of here in another two days or so. Really. I'm ahead of schedule."

"Reiko. I miss you. I hate to go to the office when I know you're not going to be there. You mean an awful lot to me, you know that?"

"I miss you, too, partner. But it won't be for long. So I got shot. So I'll be good as new. Have you touched my computer?"

"Me? I won't get within three feet of the thing. You know how I feel about that monstrosity."

"Coward. All I was going to ask is that you check the little green lights on the computer and the monitor to make sure they're off. I think I might have left it on."

"Will it shock me? Where do I turn it off."

"It *won't* shock you. And there's a little switch in the back that you just push. Someday, Riordan, I'm going to give you a lesson in how to operate a PC. It is so simple even a moron can manage it."

"Are you implying that I'm mentally defective?"

"No. You are one of the smartest people I know. About certain things. Wow!" She all but shouted that "Wow!" and I could hear a crash in the background. She muffled the phone with her hand or in her pillow, and I could dimly hear a stream of high-pitched Japanese as she apparently screamed at her mother and her uncle to shut up or get the hell out. Mama and Shiro are both Nisei, born in the U.S., but Mama learned the language of her parents along with English and she and Shiro prefer to discuss family matters in Japanese. They saw to it that Reiko and the other kids learned their mother tongue as well. I do not speak a word of the language, but sometimes you can just figure out what people are saying by the tone. Everything was quiet when she came back on the phone.

"Sorry. I had to take control a little bit. They would have had all the orderlies and nurses in the hospital in here to throw 'em out. I hear you and Balestreri cleaned up on the guys I was following. And the shyster lawyer went in the Bay. How's it coming with the Benjy Noble thing?"

"I am in a quandary, Reiko. For me, it's sort of like trying to eat squid salad with chopsticks. I get a piece just up to my mouth and it squirts off. I cannot handle your slippery stuff with chopsticks. And I cannot get a good grip on Benjy Noble. I don't even know what he looks like."

"Oh, I do. I've been reading this magazine piece. God knows I don't have much else to do right now. And daytime television is the pits, unless you like the soaps. And I don't. I just can't understand how all those pretty people can get themselves into so much trouble."

"What's the magazine? Maybe I can find a copy."

"It's called *Persona*. It's all about celebrities."

"I'll look for it. Is what you've got the current issue?"

"I think so. Let's see. Yeah, it's the one for August."

"OK, honey. Take care. And get well quick. I need you."

I got dressed and walked down to the drugstore at Ocean and Dolores and found a copy of *Persona*. I flipped through it and found the article on Benjy. "Noble Theater" it was called, a touch cute for me. It was a fair spread, with lots of pictures. And on the first page was a studio shot of Benjy Noble.

As I looked at the chubby, unlined face with the large trusting eyes, I felt they must have got a picture of the wrong guy. The expression was benign, angelic. Across from the portrait was a snapshot of Benjy with Maria Theresa O'Higgins. Now I had a point of reference. Benjy must have been about five-five, and weighed maybe 180. He had sloping shoulders and a wide waist and he made me think of Tenniel's illustration of Humpty-Dumpty in *Alice in Wonderland*. Dumpy little Benjy.

There wasn't time to read much of the text. Sally was expecting me. I turned the page. Here was Benjy at twelve or thirteen, in a military uniform. Standing behind him were Cordelia Pompilio and, I guessed, Mr. Pompilio. All three were smiling brightly.

On the opposite page was a Christmas scene, with Benjy as a very small boy. He was sitting next to the Christmas tree, holding up his favorite gift.

It was a bright red Swiss Army knife.

30
"And she's not a very good kisser."

SWISS ARMY KNIVES have been around for a long time, but I hadn't connected anything with the one found in Benjy Noble's dead throat with all the accessories pulled out until now. It had seemed like some sort of macabre joke originally. The finishing touch generated by a deranged mind.

I stuck the magazine in my coat pocket and walked up to Sally's office. She was stuffing some papers in a manila folder when I walked in the door.

"I didn't say you could take me to dinner. I thought you might be exhausted after an afternoon with Christy. You see, I'm thinking about your welfare all the time, Riordan."

"Lay off, Madame Defarge. I did not spend the afternoon with Christy. I spent most of it with Maria Theresa O'Higgins, who is far more dangerous. And I *am* pretty tired, considering that both women were intent upon dragging me into the sack, and it was all I could do to resist. I am loyal to the core—or is it 'loyal to the Corps'? But I am an ex-Army man and, despite Clint Eastwood, it was the Army, not the Marines, who did most of the fighting in Korea. But let me not digress. . . ."

"You are always digressing, Riordan. So tell me of your adventures today."

I told her about my long day, including a recap of my meeting with the two shrinks, lunch with the little teaser with the big tits, and my adventures with the black-clad barracuda who fell asleep in front of the fireplace.

"You're making this up."

"So help me, I'm not. The eminent psychiatrists weren't much help, except that Cartwright knew about the threatening letters from Paul Lindemann."

"What threatening letters?"

"I told you about the letters, dammit. Benjy apparently wrote them himself."

"Oh, yeah."

"Christy was no help at all. And she's not a very good kisser."

Sally raised her eyebrows.

"It was just a peck on the cheek, dear. No spit-swapping."

"You're vulgar, Riordan."

"Anyway, I learned only one thing from Maria Theresa. Paul Lindemann was the name of the principal character in Benjy's first Broadway play, the flop that Hal Denby invested in. The guy commits suicide in full view of the audience as the curtain comes down."

"I could have told you that. Paul Lindemann was not only the principal character. It was the name of the play. I told you I got all of Benjy's plays and read them when I found out about *Waiting for the L-Train*. I thought at the time that it must have been a real downer. Suicide is hard enough to take as an incident in a story or a play, but building sympathy for a character for two long acts, and then having that character kill himself as the play ends. Jeez! And *Paul Lindemann* was not *Anna Karenina*."

Why didn't Pam Hudson mention that fact? I thought. *She* had told me she'd read all the plays.

"What was the play about, Sal?"

"It dealt with two young gay men who lived together for a

while in what appeared to be perfect bliss. Until one of them starts a little love affair on the side. The other one kills himself. A lot of it was funny, a lot of it was very moving. But the suicide killed it. You ever see *The Boys in the Band?*"

"Yeah, in San Francisco a long time ago. What else about the play?"

"According to the notes I read, there were those who said it was autobiographical. That Benjy was the lover who strayed. That there had been a tragic suicide in his life. But you know how those things are, Pat. People will read 'autobiographical' into any piece of fiction."

"How about the other plays you read?"

"They were all very good. And very different. Benjy seemed to be interested in everything and everybody. There wasn't another play about gay people, if that's what you mean. Most of them were fairly light. Until *Memories of Jackson.* But *it* was about a man in middle age remembering an elderly black man who had been a dear friend and advisor in his childhood and teen years. It was done in flashbacks. A marvelous piece of work."

"And *Waiting for the L-Train* was about these five freaks in a subway station."

"Freaks! I hope you're kidding, Patrick. If you're not, just don't bother to ring my bell again."

"Of course, I'm kidding. So . . . you think that Benjy Noble was a truly great playwright. In a class with Arthur Miller, Thornton Wilder, Tennessee Williams. Even William Saroyan."

"Yes, I do. And Saroyan doesn't belong with that group. Except, maybe, *The Time of Your Life.* Maybe Benjy Noble hadn't quite reached his peak yet, but he was going to get there. There might have been a Nobel Prize in his future."

"That's pretty grandiose, lady. From what I saw at that rehearsal, this latest effort wasn't going to get him a trip to Stockholm."

"You exasperate me sometimes, Riordan. Let's get something to eat."

I took her to a fancy place on Ocean Avenue where the

prices are necessarily as ridiculous as the rent the place must have to pay. After a couple of vodka martinis, she calmed dow and had no difficulty putting away a filet mignon that set me back twenty-seven bucks à la carte. My hand trembled slightly when I laid my credit card on the check. I was pretty close to the limit.

I followed her out to her condo in the Valley. It was fairly late in the evening by the time we finished dinner, and traffic on the Carmel Valley Road was light.

I sat in her living room while she "got into something more comfortable." She actually said that. She has a deep and abiding affection for cliches, and uses them with great respect. I guess that's one of the things that makes me love her.

When she re-entered the room, clad in lounging pajamas, I stood up and saluted. "At ease, private," she said, pouring herself a small brandy from a crystal carafe. "Can I get you something? A 7-Up, a ginger ale? I ran out of that no-harm, no-foul beer you like to drink."

"Thanks, no. I drank a whole bottle of that fizzy stuff that restaurant serves as table water. I don't want to make a path between here and the bathroom."

She sat next to me and slid down so that her legs were stretched out on a glass coffee table, and her neck rested on the back of the soft couch. She swirled the brandy in the snifter, and took a taste. Sally had always insisted that a good brandy was her favorite aphrodisiac. She never takes much, just a splash in her glass. But it does turn her on. I speak as an eyewitness.

"Pat, do you have any idea who killed Benjy Noble? After all, you've been working on this thing for nearly two weeks. You must have turned up something that makes you suspect somebody."

"I honestly do not have enough information to suspect anybody yet. But I think I'm learning a few things about Benjy Noble. Hey, I forgot something."

I got up and went to my coat, hanging over the back of a chair, and extracted that rolled-up magazine from my pocket.

I flipped open the book to the article, "Noble Theater," and showed it to Sally.

"Look at these pictures. You met Benjy, I didn't. He looks like a cherub in this one. Here's Cordelia. I wonder why she kept her relationship with Benjy a secret when she must have known this magazine article was coming out. I suspect she might have furnished some of the pictures. And look at this shot of Benjy at Christmas. You know what kind of knife that is, don't you?"

Sally sat up and set her brandy snifter on the coffee table. "This is incredible, Riordan. Have you read any of the article yet?"

"No, as a matter of fact. Here, let me skim through it."

Most of the piece was standard celebrity crap. And accurate, as far as I could see. At least according to what I knew up to then. Then I was stopped cold by a paragraph on the same page as Benjy's Christmas picture:

Benjy lost his parents at an early age, when he was perhaps too young to realize what had happened. But possibly the greatest tragedy in Benjy Noble's life occurred when he was fourteen. His best friend, a youth from whom was inseparable, went home one night from Benjy's house, took his father's revolver to bed with him, pulled the covers over his head, put the muzzle in his mouth and pulled the trigger. The shock left Benjy scarred for life. He never got over the death of Paul Lindemann.

31
"Put a pistol in his mouth."

T HAT'S WEIRD!" said Sally

"That's impossible," I said. "Cordelia told me that Benjy was sent away to military school by her husband because he couldn't stand the kid. He even left the house when Benjy came home to visit. Either the writer made it up or Benjy was rewriting his life as a play. Also, Benjy was nine when his mother ran off. Not likely he would have been unaffected. And his father died when he was eleven. He surely must have suffered that loss. This story must be a lot of bullshit. *Or* Cordelia was lying to me."

"Cordelia wouldn't lie, Riordan. I'm pretty cynical, as you well know, but I know Cordelia. She wouldn't lie."

"So how do I get to the truth. There's got to be some kernel of reality in this Lindemann thing. It keeps popping up."

"Well, don't bother me with it tonight. I am perfectly relaxed now. And the brandy is making me horny. The thing for you to do is go back to Cordelia and put the matter up to her."

Sally did a half-roll and landed with her head in my lap.

She hooked her arm around my neck and kissed me passionately. I picked her up and carried her into the bedroom, doing serious damage to my lower back. But, what the hell, this is where you get scenes of rolling surf, underscored with swelling music. I don't mess around describing my sex life. I just live it.

Next morning, in the usual routine, I rose early and drank the last of Sally's fresh orange juice and bolted a cup of instant coffee. I had awakened thinking of the Benjy Noble-Paul Lindemann connection and lay in bed for a half hour trying to get the thing to make sense.

At the office later that morning, I telephoned Cordelia Pompilio. "This is Pat Riordan, Cordelia. Have you seen that piece in *Persona* magazine about Benjy? Must have been written a few weeks before his death."

"Yes, I have. It's just shameful. Especially that part about Benjy's being too young to remember his mother and father. That's ridiculous. I told that writer the straight truth. Where he got that awful story about a boy named Paul Lindemann, I have no idea. I knew Benjy had written a play by that name. But it wasn't about a real person, was it?"

"That's what I'm trying to find out. You told me that Mr. Pompilio had sent Benjy to a military school someplace, didn't you."

"Yes, back in Indiana. It's a fine school. Very expensive."

"Was that right after his father died?"

"No. The school wouldn't accept Benjy until he was twelve. Mr. Pompilio tried very hard to please the boy during those years after that bitch mother of his ran away. He bought him things. A bicycle. Games. Everything. But Benjy was a strange child. When he came to live with us I knew early on that he hated my husband. Though I never really knew why."

"Is that school still operating, Cordelia?"

"Oh, yes. It's one of the few left of its type, I think. Military schools fell rather out of favor during the Viet Nam war. But Caldwell is still there. Yes."

"Do you know the name of anybody back there? Somebody in the administration, maybe."

"It's been quite a while, Mr. Riordan. Let me see . . . there *was* a Colonel Marble. I always thought that name was amusing. A military man made of very hard stone, you know. Seemed so appropriate."

"Where in Indiana is this place?"

"As I remember, it's near a place called Bloomington."

"Thanks, Cordelia. I'll keep in touch."

I lost no time putting in a call to Bloomington, Indiana. I knew that Indiana University was located there but I had never heard of Caldwell Military Academy. The information service gave me a number.

The voice that answered my call sounded very military: "Caldwell Academy, may we *help* you?"

I'm not used to young male voices on switchboard duty, but I guessed it was part of the discipline.

"May I speak to Colonel Marble, please?"

"I'm sorry, sir, but Colonel Marble retired two years ago. Can someone else help you?"

"Who's in charge now? I mean who's the commanding officer?"

"Major Paige, sir. He's in his office. May I say who's calling?"

"Yes, sir. Pfc. Riordan sends his respects to the Major and would like a few moments of his time."

"Er, yes, sir." There was a muffled giggle and the hold button went down. I got about twenty seconds of a march by John Philip Sousa.

"Pfc. Riordan? Is this some kind of a gag?" The voice was moderately young and not too military.

"I'm sorry, Major. This is Pat Riordan in Monterey, California. I'm a private investigator looking into the murder of one of your former students. I need some information. Have you been at the academy long?"

"Fifteen years, Riordan. That long enough? It's not bad duty for an old soldier. Are you—were you—really a Pfc.?"

"One of the best, Major. But you don't sound old."

"Old enough for Korea, Riordan."

That made us bosom buddies. We got to comparing notes and remembering places and things and it was old home week until I realized how much the call was costing me.

"I hate to break up this nostalgia wallow, Major, but I almost forgot what I called you about. Did you know Benjy Noble."

"Oh, hell yes, Riordan. He was a fat little kid who didn't have many friends when he was here. Never gave anybody any trouble. I was absolutely flabbergasted when I heard he won a Pulitzer Prize. That's what it was, wasn't it?"

"Did he graduate from Caldwell?"

"Yes. And I think he went on to USC. He was from California, as I remember."

"One more question. Does the name Paul Lindemann mean anything to you?"

"Oh, man, that was a painful situation. Paul was a skinny, effeminate little guy. Shouldn't have been in a military school at all. As a matter of fact, Benjy Noble might have been his only friend. The kid killed himself in the dormitory. Put a pistol in his mouth. No idea where he got the gun. And, Riordan, I haven't the faintest idea why he shot himself."

I thanked the major. He had been a lot of help. Or had he? The writer of the magazine article had got his facts twisted. Or had Benjy twisted them for him? But one thing was sure. Paul Lindemann had been a real person. He had been a close friend of Benjy. And he had taken his own life for a reason or reasons yet unknown.

32
"A good, moral, churchgoing boy."

I WAS ABOUT to hang up when I realized that just knowing that Paul Lindemann had killed himself wasn't enough.

"Hold on, Major. Do you happen to remember where Lindemann was from? Or anything about his personal life?"

"Not right off. If you can wait, I'll check the old files. But it might take me a while."

"Go ahead. I'll charge the call to somebody."

"The stuff is in another room. I'm going to put you on hold. How do you like our music?"

"Toe-tapping, Major. Beats the hell out of selections from Mantovani."

It was at least fifteen minutes before he came back on the line. I was able to hear all of "Stars and Stripes Forever" and two other Sousa marches whose names I couldn't remember. Actually, I was a little disappointed when Paige's voice cut through.

"Here it is, Riordan. The kid came from a small town in Minnesota. He had no siblings. Father is listed as a minister, no denomination given. Mother designated homemaker. We

ask parents to state some kind of reason for sending the kid to
Caldwell. This is what Lindemann's father wrote: 'We want
Paul to get more confidence and self-respect. He is shy and
nervous in the presence of children his own age. We feel that
the military atmosphere can help him.' And there is something
else to play around with, a notation in the record by Captain
Ellsworth, the school physician at the time. The doc wrote:
'Strong homosexual tendencies.' Now, this is a boy's school,
Riordan. And we get 'em when they're twelve. If you know
anything about adolescent sex problems, you know that kids
go through phases. But Ellsworth probably saw something
disturbing in the Lindemann kid or he wouldn't have made
this kind of notation."

"It's not surprising, Major. Benjy was openly gay in his
mature years. I guess the good doctor missed that one, eh?
Have you got an address for the parents in Minnesota?"

Paige gave me what he had on the record. "It's very old.
God knows if they're still there. But good luck if you mean to
try to get in touch with them."

I expressed my gratitude again to Major Paige for his help
and finally ended the call. I was afraid to add up the minutes
that had gone by but I was already thinking I could charge
them to Braverman's insurance company. A call to Indiana
might be hard to explain to Hal Denby.

But I wasn't through. I got through to the directory assistance operator in the Minnesota town where the Lindemanns
had lived. Yes, there was a Reverend Lindemann listed at the
same address. I was given a number.

A woman answered at the Lindemann residence. She had a
faint Northern European accent, German or Scandinavian.
"This is Mrs. Lindemann. Who's calling, please?"

I explained who I was and what my mission was. There
was tension in her voice when she spoke again. "You must
realize, Mr. Riordan, that Paul's death was a great tragedy in
our lives. It has been many years, but we still bear the grief as
if it were yesterday. To have to discuss it with a perfect
stranger is very painful."

"I'm sorry, Mrs. Lindemann, but I'm trying to find out if Paul's death has any connection at all with the death of Benjy Noble."

There was a silence. Then, "You'll have to talk to the Reverend Lindemann. We feel that Benjy Noble was directly responsible for Paul's suicide. But a woman cannot talk about such things. My husband will be home in an hour or so. I will tell him of your call. Please leave your number."

"Can't I reach him somewhere, Mrs. Lindemann. I don't want to burden you with an expensive long distance call."

"No. I must talk to him first. Then he will call you. If he thinks it's appropriate."

It was a tantalizing but most unsatisfactory conversation. Paul Lindemann's mother could speak of his death only reluctantly and with great pain. I was convinced when she hung up that the Reverend would never call me back.

But an hour later, the phone rang. "Mr. Riordan, this is Edgar Lindemann. My wife has told me of your call. Why do you think Benjamin Noble's death could be connected to the suicide of my son?"

That was the first time anybody had referred to Benjy as Benjamin. The Reverend Lindemann had a strong preacher's voice and he might have been in the next room, rather than a small town in Minnesota.

"I really don't know, Reverend. I'm just looking for fragments of Benjy's life and Paul's name came up. Is there anything you can tell me?"

"First let me assure you that I have not left this town in twenty years, a fact which hundreds of people can verify. If you suspect me or Mrs. Lindemann of killing Noble, you may put your mind at rest."

"There was no such thought in my mind, Reverend. I was just—"

"Picking up the pieces? Well, you should know this: I have always held Benjamin Noble responsible for the death of my son. Paul wrote me a letter and posted it before he took his own life. He was a good boy, Mr. Riordan. A good, moral, churchgoing boy. Benjamin Noble had befriended him when he went to Caldwell. Paul had never had many friends. But the 'friendship' degenerated into a homosexual relationship. And Noble soon tired of Paul and turned to others. Poor Paul. He was never strong. The guilt of this sinful attachment and the loss of it were too much. He took his own life. And Benjamin Noble was to blame. I must confess that I rejoiced in the news of Noble's death. It is unworthy of a minister of the gospel. 'Vengeance is mine, saith the Lord.' "

I thanked Reverend Lindemann for his help. It was clear that neither he nor his wife had beaten Benjy to death and left his body on the Forest Theater stage with a knife in his throat. Although it seemed to them a case of justifiable homicide.

Benjy's obsession with having killed somebody was explained. The letters he wrote to himself, probably in a fit of depression, were explained. I envisioned the playwright drinking alone, late at night, remembering Paul, writing pages of gibberish, actually believing that his new play was plagiarized. Well, maybe it was. Maybe it came out of a youthful discussion years before. But I came to a conclusion on one very important point:

Although the suicide of Paul Lindemann weighed heavily on Benjy, it had nothing to do with his murder.

33

"You're watchin' the menagerie."

HAVING SPENT the greater part of the morning in touch
with middle America, I decided to take a walk in the cool
Monterey Bay air. The papers for days had been full of the
interminable heat wave that was stifling places like Bloomington, Indiana, and Whatsitsname, Minnesota. You and I know
that the oppressive humid heat of the great midwest cannot
travel through telephone lines, but I could sense the temperature in the voices of the people I had been talking with.

Actually I had been in Central Indiana in the summertime
many years ago with my parents on a visit to some long forgotten kin. I was only five or six years old, but I remember
that trip well. It was in the days before anybody got the idea
to air condition automobiles. Maybe they thought it couldn't
be done. And cooling systems weren't all that efficient, either.
My dad had to stop every couple of hundred miles or so on
the trip across country to replenish the water in the radiator.
He swore he'd never make a journey like that again. As I
recall, it was my mother's relatives we were visiting. Maybe
that had something to do with it.

I blessed the fog as I walked down Alvarado Street toward the Bay. I was wearing an old gray wool sweater with the elbows out that hung on a peg in the office. Reiko had tried to throw it away a couple of times, but I caught her. "It's a disgrace," she'd say. "It's comfortable, by God," I'd tell her.

Picking up my pace, I crossed Del Monte and walked through the Doubletree Inn. My trained observer's instincts told me that there was no convention in town. Not a soul in the lobby with a tag on his or her bosom. You know, "HELLO, I'm Esther Goldthwait from Pocatello." People actually wander around town with those things on 'em. Out behind the hotel there are some historic buildings just before you get to Fisherman's Wharf. An organ grinder was attracting the usual crowd of kids with his monkey. The sea lions were honking at the far end of the wharf where tourists were tossing fish scraps into the Bay. A very old man sat on a piling, hunched over, arms folded, wearing an ancient pea jacket. I approached him.

"How's it going?" I asked, just to be friendly. He lifted a weatherbeaten face and fixed bright blue eyes on me, probably wondering for an instant if I were a tourist who had at first mistaken him for a wood carving. Seeing the sweater with the frayed elbows, he smiled.

"You're doin' what I'm doin', ain't you. You're watchin' the menagerie. You live in this town, don't you?"

"Carmel. I have an office up on Alvarado. I was sitting up there alone getting cabin fever, so I decided to take a walk. Menagerie?"

"The tourists, young fella. Ever see so many fat asses in your life? Especially them women with the real short shorts, with their cheeks hangin' out. Boy, you got to have a real good ass to get away with that. And would you look at the gut on that big guy over there. The one with the T-shirt and the plaid shorts. Where do they come from? Do they think Monterey is Miami Beach?"

"They bring money, skipper. The life blood of the Peninsula. Without them, only the rich could live here. Look at this string of restaurants, big ones and little ones, and all doing good business. And the people in 'em don't know a bay salmon from a rock cod. Most of 'em don't know *what* calamari is. But they pay the prices, even when the coffee is weak and the bread is stale."

The old man wiped his nose with the back of his hand. "That's real sad. I used to fish here when it was a respectable profession and a real good living when they were runnin'. But that's all gone. Like the real good restaurants. I guess you're too young to remember the one that used to be right here at the shore end of the Wharf. Palermo II it was called, run by an Eye-talian guy lived over in Salinas. Had great fish dinners, but Eye-talian food that was the best I ever eat. God *damn*, that was a good place."

"The guy's name was Pompilio, wasn't it?" I asked, feeling pretty good for having been addressed as "young fella."

"Why, yes it was. But the place burned down twenty, twenty-five years ago? How old did you say you were?"

"Plenty old enough, skipper. Do you remember anything about the fire?"

"Sure do. Watched it burn. Nobody knew it at the time, but ol' Pompilio was in the building when the fire started. Upstairs in the office, countin' his money. Arsonist done the job. I guess when he finally smelled the smoke, ol' Pompilio was trapped up there. Nobody heard him yell, though. That's what folks thought was funny. There was people all around, but nobody heard him yell."

"Did they ever catch the guy who started the fire?"

"Nope, not as I recollect. Got away clean as a whistle."

"Well, did anybody come up with any *reasons* for arson. Did Pompilio have enemies? Somebody else in the restaurant business?"

"It's been a while. My memory ain't as good as it used to be. As I remember now, Pompilio was pretty well liked. Good man. His wife's still around. Don't think they had any kids."

I thanked the old man and wished him a long life. He nodded and waved a thin, knobby hand. I continued my walk to the end of the pier. The fat, sassy sea lions were playing their little game with the tourists, gorging themselves on fish scraps. These guys never had to forage for a living and they looked it. Full of blubber, they just lounged around the Wharf and waited for the folks who paid fifty cents for a little cardboard tray of stuff the fishmarkets would otherwise throw away.

There was a good breeze off the Bay and my head was clearing nicely. I had finally got Indiana and Minnesota out of my system. I stopped and got a portable crabmeat cocktail and ate it slowly as I walked back to the shore end. The old fisherman was gone when I passed his roost. The organ grinder's monkey was accepting coins from delighted children and tipping his little bellboy's cap. I began to feel almost cheerful.

I was walking back through the lobby of the Doubletree Inn when somebody called to me. "Mr. Riordan. Hello."

I turned to see Pam Hudson approaching. "I thought you had gone back to San Jose."

She smiled. "That's what I intended to do after Dr. Cartwright left. But the weather was so nice here. And I haven't had a vacation for a couple of years. It seems that every time I get ready to take a trip, one of my patients has a crisis. I'm ashamed to say so but this is my first trip to the Monterey Peninsula. Is there anything I should see? Anything special?"

I began the standard itinerary: The adobes and other historical monuments of Monterey, the Monterey Bay Aquarium, the Seventeen-Mile Drive, the Lighthouse in Pacific Grove, Tor House in Carmel, Clint Eastwood's house in Carmel (I just happen to know where it is), Point Lobos, the Highlands, maybe Big Sur. "You pick up what's left of Cannery Row when you go to the Aquarium. Ever read Steinbeck?"

"In school, years ago. I guess everybody does."

"Not enough nowadays. Hey, if you'll walk back up to my office with me, I'll take you on the short but comprehensive guided tour. Maybe along the way we could talk a little more about Benjy Noble."

34

"Come in out of the dark, Sean."

MAYBE I SHOULDN'T have said that. About Benjy
Noble, I mean. Dr. Hudson fell silent, but smiled faintly and
fell in alongside me for the walk up Alvarado Street. She
remained very quiet as I drove her around the streets of
Monterey pointing out the old adobes and the house where
Robert Louis Stevenson is said to have spent his very brief
visit to the town. "I won't bother with the stuff around
Fisherman's Wharf. You're close enough to walk from your
hotel. You are staying at the Doubletree?"

She nodded, but her smile seemed forced.

We were moping along Ocean View Boulevard in Pacific
Grove when I decided to drive out on one of the vista parking
lots and stop. "You're not really enjoying this, are you?" I
asked. "The fact that it is a beautiful day doesn't seem to matter to you. The fact that people come thousands of miles for
this scenery doesn't appear to impress you. What's up?"

"I'm sorry, Mr. Riordan. I was feeling pretty chipper when
we met in the hotel lobby. Dr. Cartwright and I had a long
talk, and I was certain that the Benjy Noble case was finished.

But there was something that Cartwright said that bothered me. He hadn't said anything during our conversations on the phone, and I don't remember seeing anything in his notes. But Cartwright felt strongly that Benjy was desperately seeking a father image. He said he felt it in Benjy's attachment for him. I knew that Benjy's mother had abandoned him when he was nine and his father died a couple of years later. But it was my impression that his aunt and uncle had been very generous and had raised him like their own child. When Cartwright told me this morning that Benjy had confessed to him that his uncle hated his guts, and that Benjy was terrified of his uncle, I began to wonder. I got the name of Benjy's aunt and telephoned her. She told me her husband died in a fire that destroyed one of his restaurants."

I nodded. "And the same thought crossed your mind that crossed mine when I heard about the fire. Uncle hates Benjy, Benjy hates uncle. Benjy knows that uncle is in the building, sets fire, destroys uncle. So, instead of a guilt complex resulting from Paul Lindemann's suicide, we have a guilt complex stemming from the murder of Mr. Pompilio. Tell me, did Benjy ever say anything to you that might have suggested what his problem was all about?"

"Never. I told you that in the beginning. He would close his eyes, clench his fists, and whisper: 'I killed him, I killed him.' I'd ask him to explain. 'Who was it, Benjy. Whom did you kill?' He'd just look away from me and remain silent. When our time was up, he'd get up and walk out the door without a word."

"Has Cartwright left town?"

"I believe he had a flight out to L.A. early this morning. He had to make a speech before a group down there."

"Do you know where he's staying?"

"No. I had no occasion to ask. Why?"

"I don't really know. I just think he might know something else—some little kernel of information—that might give us a key to Benjy Noble's state of mind. Something that would furnish a hint as to just what in Benjy's past—or recent—life got him killed."

I did not relish the idea of calling all the hotels in Los Angeles County to find Dr. Charles Cartwright. Even if I limited it to the expensive ones. "Oh, well, forget it, Doctor. Let's see the sights."

I hit all the highlights of the Monterey Peninsula, ending late in the afternoon at the Highlands Inn where I treated my guest to a tall one as we watched the sun set in the Pacific. I couldn't help wondering, though, which of the people at the front desk were Sally Morse's spies. Here I sat with this tall, beautiful psychiatrist gazing at one of the most romantic vistas on the Pacific Coast, if not in the world, and I felt fidgety because I *knew* it would get back to Sal.

We drove up the coast in the fading light and I deposited Dr. Hudson at her hotel. She told me she had enjoyed the tour, but had made up her mind to check out the next day. "It's *my* guilt this time, Mr. Riordan. Do you remember Mitzi, the little girl who was bawling in my office when you were there? She's been calling the office constantly since I came down here. She needs me. And whether her fears are imaginary or not, I'd better get up to San Jose to be available. Ellen—my assistant or *bodyguard,* if you will—said Mitzi sounded pretty distraught when she called. Thanks so much for all your trouble. And keep in touch. I'd like to know how all this turns out."

"You might think of doing the same for me. If you remember anything you think might give us a lead, I'd be deeply grateful."

I drove out Pacific to its dead end at Soledad, cut out to Munras to catch the highway over Carmel Hill. Night was beginning to darken the narrow streets of Carmel, the only city in the world that I know where a motorist has to use his high beams to get around after dark. It's the only way to read the street signs. I pulled into my driveway at Sixth and Santa Rita and walked around to the front door. There's this weird thing about my back door. It locks from inside with a dead bolt, but there's no keyhole on the outside. So I either have to leave it unlocked or walk around. But I need the exercise.

It's really black as pitch after dark at my front door. I have to feel for the lock, but I'm used to it. There was a surprise waiting for me on this occasion, however. While I was fumbling with my key, a voice came out of the blackness to my left. "I've been waiting for you, Riordan. Why don't you get better chairs for your deck. I nearly went through this one."

I ducked instinctively, opened the door, and flicked on the light switch inside. In the dim light that filtered out, I could make out the figure of a man walking toward me with his hands thrust deep in the pockets of his pants. "Hey, I'm not going to hit you or anything, Riordan. It's me, Sean. The career busboy."

I was relieved to hear his voice. In spite of the fact that my profession leads me into dangerous situations now and then, and despite warnings from my friends in law enforcement, I have no gun around the house. As a matter of fact, the only weapon I ever use is a blackthorn walking stick, but I keep that in the office. I know I can't do a hell of a lot of damage with it, but it gives me a sense of security. You already know I have this thing about guns. It all goes back to those days when I slept with my M-1 in Korea. Bullets are very hard, and they have a serious effect on human flesh when the two meet. I had seen enough—maybe caused enough. But, like the gal sings in that song, I'm still here.

"Come in out of the dark, Sean. I should have known you. There's the distinct smell of garlic and cooking grease in the air. Where are you working now? Steak house? I know it's not Chinese. They use peanut oil."

"I'm grilling hamburgers at a fast-food joint until I can get back to my career busing dishes. God, those things smoke up the place. Smells good on the outside. They want it that way. Brings the customers in. But the burgers aren't that good."

"What do you want here, Sean? I thought we had everything on the table. Are you going to confess to the murder of Benjy Noble?"

"Hell, no, Riordan, I didn't kill the little bastard. But I've got a pretty good idea who did."

35

"Gerald Stone is what he's known by."

Y OU'RE GOING to tell me Honest Abe Atterbury collared
you on the street and confessed he did the bloody murder
with a pickax or something, aren't you? Or do you think one
of the cast members lured Benjy to the theater in the middle
of the night and bludgeoned him to death? If so, that bit with
the Swiss Army knife was a neat afterthought. Like a mara-
schino cherry on a sundae."

"No, Riordan, I'm not the dumb shit you think I am. I
really do have some information for you. Of course, if you're
not interested, I'll just be on my way."

I looked for a long time at Sean Wetherby's pimply face.
It's true, I didn't really trust the guy. That's probably not fair.
But Sean just has this sneaky, oily look about him. I thought
at the time that if the kid ever did get a break in the movies,
he'd probably play one of the bad guys. A lot of movie bad
guys are really pussycats, but they have the look.

"Come on in and sit down. What do you know? I'm going
into the kitchen to make myself a sandwich, but keep talking.
It's just that I haven't eaten since breakfast and I'm starving to

death." I threw open the refrigerator and withdrew a block of swiss cheese and some mayonnaise along with one of my favorite fake beers. "Which of our good friends did the dastardly deed?"

"Nobody you know, Riordan. But there's this guy I had acting classes with up at the college. He's a big burly guy, but one of *those,* know what I mean? A Tinker Bell."

"Go ahead."

"He tried out for a part in the show when the first call went out. I think he got one call-back, but he didn't make the cut. Benjy went out of his way to be nice to the guy because, well, they were kindred spirits, you might say. Even after the casting was done, I saw this guy with Benjy a couple of times in two different restaurants I was working in. Guy calls himself Gerald Stone, but it's not his right name. Last time I saw the two of them together, they looked pretty chummy."

"You're saying that Benjy Noble's death was due to a violent lovers' quarrel. They had a tryst at the Forest Theater and it wound up with Noble beaten to death. Why the touch with the knife?"

"Oh, God, I don't know. You figure that one out. But I think I've got something."

"Why hasn't this guy come into the picture until now? Don't the police know about him? And why didn't they have their little rendezvous somewhere else."

"Noble was staying with Hal Denby, remember. And maybe they didn't have the price of a Carmel motel."

"That is pure bullshit, Sean. Benjy had plenty of money. If he wanted to entertain this guy he could have got a suite at the Monterey Plaza. Give me something more."

Wetherby seemed to lose some of his initial enthusiasm. His voice dropped a few decibels and he began picking his fingernails. "Look, Riordan, I didn't like Benjy Noble. I don't like this Stone dude. But I'm saying there's the possibility. And Stone is a really big mother. You wouldn't think a guy who looks like that could be a faggot, would you?"

"Some of the hairiest, ugliest, beefiest guys in the NFL

have been gay, Sean. Looks don't mean a thing. But, tell you what I'll do: I'll look into this thing about . . . what's his name again?"

"Gerald Stone is what he's known by. He told me it was fake but that he wanted something that sounded really butch. You know, like Rock Hudson."

"Know where I can find him?"

"I know where he works." Wetherby gave me an address in Monterey on Calle Principal. "It's a computer store. The guy is something of a hacker."

"I'll look him up. Meanwhile, where can I find you?"

"I'm starting a new job tomorrow. Real fancy restaurant on Ocean Avenue. Even a bus has got to wear a black bow tie."

I opened the door and Sean disappeared into the darkness. There was a stiff breeze up from the bay and I could hear the surf pound. The cheese in my sandwich was pretty dry. The mayonnaise didn't help much and the french bun I had the stuff on was maybe five days old. Three or four bites had shredded my gums and I didn't feel like eating any more. Fortunately, there was a pint of cheap vanilla ice cream in the freezer to soothe my sore mouth.

Slouching on the couch with the carton of ice cream in one hand and a soup spoon in the other, I tried to relax. It's no fun being alone at my age. Oh, sure, I like restful solitude from time to time. Everybody does. But being alone is intolerable. Sally lives alone and seems to thrive on it. But, hell, she usually gets home late, spends her evenings getting ready for the next day, goes to bed and gets up again. I just sort of rattle around in the house.

I picked up the remote gadget and pointed it at the TV, flipping through the channels in numerical sequence until I came to what looked like a detective story of some sort. These fearless guys with chiseled profiles who chase down the criminals fascinate me. That is, until a couple of the real bad guys, who have been following the detective for no explainable reason, trap our hero and beat up on him. One of them always holds him and the other one lands fearsome punches in his gut. But we know, don't we, that he'll catch up and get his revenge, even though we see him with a trickle of blood at the corner of his mouth and a nasty bruise high on his left cheek. Then there's got to be a chase. There comes a point in all of these things when the people run out of conversation and they start chasing each other and ruin a lot of late model automobiles.

I had not intended to finish the ice cream, but I did. Then I caught the 10 o'clock news, and dragged myself up to the bedroom.

At the top of the stairs I got the distinct feeling that I was not alone. Only the bathroom light was on so I couldn't see all that clearly, but there was a lump in my bed. My eyes began to accustom themselves to the dim light, and I saw feminine undergarments hanging over the back of a chair. In my bathroom a freshly laundered pair of pantyhose hung neatly on the shower curtain rod. It's not that I'm not used to a woman in my bed, but this was really something of a surprise. I succumbed to my first instinct and made my very worst mistake.

"Christy?" I called. Something had suggested to me that little miss hotbox had snuck into my bedchamber. Must have been a nasty piece of wishful thinking.

The figure in the bed sat up abruptly. "Riordan, you sonofabitch. Here I think I have a nice surprise for you and you're thinking about that little slut." It was, of course, Sally Morse, who has the only other key to my house.

The situation called for some pretty quick thinking and persuasion. "Sal, why did you do this to me? The charming young lady you have just maligned has been trying to put the make on me, but I have resisted nobly. It's just that I thought she had me trapped this time."

I turned on the light. Sally looked as if she could cheerfully strangle me. She sat bolt upright. One shoulder strap of her nightgown had slipped intriguingly low. Her hair was fanned around her face, and she looked absolutely gorgeous. The swiss cheese turned to stone in my stomach.

"Why should I believe you?" she asked. "Maybe you're used to finding Christy Burgess in your bed. Maybe that's where you've been. In Christy's bed. You better watch out, Riordan. Keep it up and you'll die in the saddle. Unless I kill you first."

"It's the God's truth, Sal, I have never even so much as patted the lady's fanny. I am true blue, believe me."

Her face softened. I sat down on the bed and took her hand. She still looked at me accusingly, and her lower lip stuck out like Jackie Cooper's.

"I've been trying to get in touch with you all day. And then Terry Jerome phoned to tell me that she saw you with a tall, beautiful woman at the Highlands Inn. Terry's on the front desk there evenings. I sort of thought that it was business, because I didn't think you'd two-time me with a woman who is taller than you are. I tried to get you at the office, even left messages on your answering machine. Finally, in desperation I came up here. My car's parked out front, on Santa Rita. Funny you didn't see it."

"You know I park in the driveway off Sixth Avenue. I couldn't see anything until I got in the house. But why was it so important that you see me tonight?"

Sally squeezed my hand. Suddenly it was as if she had never been angry. "You've got to be careful, Pat. I have a feeling that this thing's a long way from being over, and you might be in danger if you get too close to the truth, whatever it is. I talked to Hal Denby today. He told me his life had been threatened."

36
"You had a nightgown on."

I ALWAYS LIKE IT better when Sally sleeps over at *my* house. She sort of likes it, too, although it'd be tough to get her to admit it. At my place she's only a few short blocks from her office, so she can stay in the sack as long as she wants to. On the other hand, she always bitches because she doesn't have the right clothes in my closet. She keeps enough stuff here so that I had to buy a wardrobe to hang my own clothes in, but she never has the right dress, or anything else.

My biological clock, which is running down altogether too swiftly, is set for six in the A.M. and often the inner alarm goes off earlier. There is no point, I tell myself, in letting the days go by any faster than they do already, and sleeping just eats up a lot of precious time. But I better get on with it before I burst into a chorus of "September Song."

Sally's report that Hal Denby's life had been threatened was sort of underwhelming to me. Denby was not my favorite person, and I suspected from the beginning that he knew more than he was telling about Benjy's death. I was pretty certain that he was holding back something from the time he

169

showed me the letters from Benjy's briefcase. And since the episode of the letters, I had learned that Denby knew damn well who Paul Lindemann was. At least, he should have remembered the name of the play. Yet he said nothing when he handed me the letters. He *wanted* me to believe that the threat was real, that the writer was a genuine suspect in Benjy Noble's murder.

Then there was Denby's connection with Pam Hudson. Something was going on there. The two were altogether too chummy when I left them in the cocktail lounge in San Jose. And there was his involvement with the early Noble plays and the good Dr. Cartwright, the overweight shrink from New York.

I sat at the tiny table in the dining nook of my kitchen sipping a cup of coffee and mulling over all the bits and pieces of information I had on why Benjy Noble was killed and who might have done it. So many people had a relationship with Denby. He began to be the central character in my drama, looming in the background in every move that anybody made. But what reason could he have had for wanting Benjy Noble dead?

Sally appeared in the doorway with a face full of sleep. Funny, for a lady of mature years, she looks pretty damn good in the morning without any makeup. Sally has a lot of gray in her dark auburn hair, but she has the kind of skin that will remain unlined into her seventies if she takes good care of it. I got up and poured her a cup of coffee.

"What time is it?" she asked. "You don't have anything upstairs but a clock radio that says 3 P.M., and I know it's not three in the afternoon. The sun is hardly up yet."

"It's quarter to seven, my love. Drink this. Want some juice?"

"How long has it been in your refrigerator?"

She had me there. I make my orange juice from the frozen cylinders you find in the markets, but I only drink enough to get the film off my teeth in the morning. Often it begins to ferment in the container.

"You've got me there." I peered into the fridge and observed that there was little more than an inch and a half in the bottom of the juice bottle. "But now that you mention it, I suspect you could get a little buzz on with what's left."

"Just coffee. And don't try to palm off any of your stale cereal. Or your sour milk. Got any bread?"

"There's some in the freezer, I think. Toaster still works. But you'll have to eat it dry. There's some peanut butter, but I got a knife stuck in it and it won't come out."

"Forget it, Riordan. Coffee is fine. I'll stop by Wishart's on the way to the office and get a sticky bun. Why in God's name don't you keep some decent edible stuff around?"

"You want to be my housekeeper? I can't afford one, and I've asked you more than once. Reiko is as bad as you are. Even worse. That one has a mean streak when it comes to prescribing for me. And neither one of you will live with me. Maybe I should ask Christy. . . ."

"Mention that name again and I will carve you up on the spot. You do have a sharp knife around, don't you?"

"So sue me. Sally, you came here last evening and fell asleep in my bed."

"I was listening to a radio talk show until it bored the hell out of me, so I turned it off and slipped under the covers to take a nap."

"You had a nightgown on."

"That was for your benefit. You weren't going to kick me out of bed, were you?"

"What I can't understand is why you didn't hear me talking with Sean Wetherby downstairs. And then I watched TV for a couple of hours."

"I did hear you come in, and I did hear Sean. I felt it best to stay up here. Didn't want to soil my reputation. I guess I fell asleep by the time you turned on the television."

"Let's get back to Hal Denby's death threat. All you told me last night was that he had received several telephone calls from an unidentified male. Sure it was a male?"

"Denby told me that a man called him and admitted

killing Benjy Noble. He then proceeded to tell Hal that he was next on the list. All I know is that Hal *says* it was a man."

"Did he tell anybody else?"

"My God, Riordan, how should I know? Hal called me at my office in a kind of a swivet and told me about the threatening calls. He didn't tell me how many others he had told, and I didn't ask him. But I thought I ought to tell you. Maybe he called your office, but you were showing that tall, skinny head doctor around town. Maybe he called me because he knew I'd tell you."

"Why don't you go back to bed, Sal? This is the middle of the night for you. You'll never make it through the day if you stay up. Look, it's just five after seven."

She gave me a look that could have penetrated the flesh if I hadn't ducked. "You are the most unfeeling, frustrating, totally irritating man in the world, Riordan. Here I am, with hardly a change of clothes, without a hair dryer—"

"Oh, I've got a hair dryer. I use it to dry out the distributor on the Mercedes on foggy mornings. Learned the trick from Greg Farrell."

"—*without* a hair dryer, with only the makeup I carry in my purse. I made a great sacrifice to bring you what I thought was some significant information. . . ."

"Because you wanted to sleep with me. Sally, I love you. Marry me."

"*No,* you miserable bastard. Well, maybe next year. In the spring."

She jumped from her chair into my lap, and I kissed her mightily, ignoring the upset coffee cup on my table and the hot liquid dripping on my knees.

"Does that mean yes?" I asked, as the pain of the spilled coffee reached my brain.

"Call me next week," she said, scrambling from my lap, hitching up her gown and running up the stairs.

I slipped a slice of frozen bread into the toaster and struggled to remove the knife from the peanut butter which was about as easy as extracting Excalibur from the stone.

The phone chirped. My home phone chirps. It's the office phone that bleats. I'm going to get a couple of phones that ring.

"It's Hal Denby, Riordan. I don't know how to tell you this. It has shaken me up considerably, but. . . .

"Your life has been threatened. You've been getting calls. It's seven-thirty in the morning. What do you think I can do about it?"

"That's a pretty callous attitude. I imagine Sally told you about the calls. But my life is in danger, Riordan, I'm sure of it. I was awakened by my doorchime this morning. I'm a light sleeper. My man answered the door and found a small package on the doorstep. He brought it to me immediately."

"That wasn't too cool, Denby. Lots of big explosions come in small packages."

"I know, I know. I wasn't thinking. It wasn't an explosive."

"So what was it? I'm burning with curiosity."

"It was a knife, Riordan. A Swiss Army knife. With all the blades and accessories pulled out. Just like the one the police found in Benjy Noble's throat."

37
"But Hal is a bit of a shit, too."

SALLY CAME down the stairs, muttering to herself, grimacing at her reflection in a window. "I look like a bag lady this morning, Riordan. How can I face my upscale clientele looking like this?"

To me she looked like a *Vogue* ad. Her hair was perfectly coiffed, her dress was in the vanguard of fashion, her face was positively beautiful.

"Maybe you ought to stay here hiding all day, Sal. You look like something the cat dragged in."

She sniffed. She had been fishing for a compliment, and she hooked an old shoe. Sally is always acutely aware of how she looks. She knew she was a stunner that morning, and she wasn't going to leave the house without some acknowledgement. She gave me another of her patented dagger looks. So I backed off.

"You know damn well you're gorgeous, lady. You couldn't be anything else after spending the night with a stud like me." I expanded my chest and flexed my biceps.

"You were good for about twenty minutes, macho man,

and then you went to sleep. And you snored. Who was that on the phone?"

"Denby. Somebody sent him a little present. A nicely packaged Swiss Army knife. You get the connection, of course."

"Not really. Sounds sort of fishy to me. I've often wondered about that knife thing. The way I get it, Benjy was probably dead before somebody stuck it in him. Some sort of symbolism involved, I guess."

"You mean like the murderer was really a member of the Swiss Army? I don't know if there is a Swiss Army. I know the Vatican Guard is made up of Swiss by tradition. But I seriously doubt that Benjy was done in by a monsignor. I'm quite sure there isn't a Swiss Navy. The knife might be a red herring. At least, the color is appropriate."

"I'm getting out of here. Call me if you find out anything. We're supposed to rehearse at Maria Theresa's house this evening."

"I was wondering. How does Sean ever make rehearsals? He's always messing up dining rooms and fracturing crockery in the evening."

"Not always. He just takes off whatever job he's on at the time. Remember, there are 700 eating places on and around the Peninsula, and Sean has only used up thirty or forty of them. Check the want-ads in *The Herald*. They're always looking for restaurant workers."

She kissed me gently on the cheek to avoid smearing her lipstick, and turned to leave.

"Sally. How much do you know about Harold Denby? I mean, about the man's private life. He's married, isn't he?"

"He is *indeed* married to the former Lillian Delahanty, daughter of an affluent Massachusetts politician. I've set up trips for them many times. They have two children, both grown, of course. The son is the older. He's a physician in the East someplace. The daughter lives in L.A. I don't know much about her."

"It's an old marriage, then?"

"Long time, Riordan. However, people tell me that Hal

likes to explore the greener grass fairly frequently. Lillian is a little older than he is, and somewhat hooked on booze, as I understand it. Sips all day, you know. Not the best of company. But Hal is a bit of a shit, too. Lillian inherited a lot of money from her grandfather. That's what got Hal started in business. He's been good at it, but he would never have got off the ground without Lillian's inheritance."

It was actually more information than I had expected from Sally. But she's worked with the cream of society of the Monterey Peninsula for twenty years, and is a veritable encyclopedia of gossip.

"Gotta go," she said. "Goodbye, stud."

I waved at her as she went out the door. What a woman, I thought. Sometimes I wonder what she sees in an old infantryman like me. I must be pretty goddam charming.

The phone made its obnoxious sound again. It was Reiko. "I'm going home today. Thought you'd like to know. The doctor says I'm making remarkable progress and should be back in the office in no more than two weeks. Maybe there's something I can do when I'm home. I hate daytime TV, and if I'm not busy I'll have to listen to my mother all day."

"Tell you what. When you get settled in, call the office of Charles Cartwright in New York. He was Benjy Noble's resident Broadway shrink. Try to find out where he's staying in Los Angeles. Then put a call in to Cartwright. When you get him, ask him if he remembers anything Benjy might have told him about a Swiss Army knife. I'll pay for the calls. We got a nice fee and percentage from Braverman on the Talbott case. There's at least enough for the rent and next month's salary for you."

"You think I *live* on what you pay me? If my Grandpa-san hadn't left me a lot of money, I'd have starved to death by now. But OK, I'll get on the phone this afternoon. Mama doesn't like telephones. She'll leave me alone."

"Call me if you find out anything. I'll either be here or at the office."

I shaved and took a shower, remembering to open the

bathroom window. Recently, I've noticed that the guy next door has positioned his potted plants below my bathroom window to take advantage of the spray. We have water problems in California, you know.

When I got to my office in Monterey, Harold Denby was pacing back and forth in front of my door.

"You take your own sweet time getting to business, Riordan. I'd never have made it if I had been as lackadaisical as you are."

I told you the guy was a stickler for punctuality. But, hell, I hadn't made an appointment with him. He just showed up.

"Come on in," I said, opening the door. "What else has happened? More phone calls, more packages?"

"I just thought you should see this." He held up an open box containing the knife he had received that morning. It was an ordinary boring model, lacking toothpick and tweezers.

"What am I supposed to do with it? You should take it to the Sheriff's office. There might be fingerprints."

"Oh, sure. Mine. And my man's. We both handled the thing before we thought about fingerprints."

"So here it is. Nothing extraordinary. Simple knife. Two blades. Screwdriver. Can opener. Corkscrew and punch on the other side."

"Look at it closely, Riordan. It's old. The blades are stained. There's an accumulation of pocket lint in the grooves. The loop on the end is rusty. This knife is old. And look at this."

He turned the knife over. Beneath the familiar shield-and-cross trade mark, in very fine silver inlay was the name "Benjy."

38
"I considered him to be a friend."

Benjy's own knife. The one he was holding up so proudly in the Christmas picture from long ago. I took it from Denby and examined it closely. Little nicks and scratches in the red body. Little spots of rust at the bases of the blades. An unevenness along the business edges of the blades that indicated the use of a sharpener, perhaps more often than really necessary. These instruments are beautifully made. I had one for a long time myself, until it slipped through a hole in my pocket and was gone forever. I mourned the loss of that knife for months. And that was only a couple of years ago. The hole is still in the pants pocket. I just don't put anything in it anymore.

I rummaged under a stack of rumpled newspapers and brought out my copy of *Persona* magazine. I held it up to Denby. "Ever seen this?"

"Yes. Benjy had an advance copy a month before he died. We went over it together. This was just after he arrived in California to supervise *Waiting for the L-Train*. He told me a lot of the stuff in the article was inaccurate, to say the least.

He spent about an hour with the writer and suggested that she contact Cordelia Pompilio. Benjy appeared to be amused by the pictures Cordelia gave the writer. Especially the Christmas one where he's holding the knife. He said something funny at the time. Something about . . . I think he used the words 'vindictive old woman.'"

"That doesn't sound like the sweet, lovable Benjy Noble I've been hearing about since you got me on this case. What could he possibly have meant?"

"As I remember it, he got the knife as a present from Mr. Pompilio one Christmas before his father died. He was about nine, I think. It was the first Christmas after his mother had run off. Benjy was pretty vague about the knife and what Cordelia was 'vindictive' about. He said something about having damaged something of hers."

"Where's the damn thing been all this time. And why should it be sent to you. Does any of this make sense?"

I looked closely at Denby. The usually dignified and controlled man of business had been disturbed by the arrival of the knife. He had left his house without shaving and without a necktie. In a man like Harold Denby, that is gross negligence.

"It's crazy, Riordan. I was a great admirer of Noble's talent. I considered him to be a friend. It seemed to me a great coup to be able to bring his new play to Carmel, even under a *nom de plume*. He seemed a little strange to me at times, but I just charged that up to the creative mind at work. I knew he was homosexual, but that didn't bother me. Benjy never tried to put a move on me. When Cartwright called and asked me if I could recommend a psychiatrist he could consult out here, I immediately thought of Pam Hudson. That's all. That's my whole involvement. I cannot conceive of any reason anyone might have for threatening my life."

I took advantage of the opening. "What's your relationship with Pam Hudson?"

Denby's face reddened. "I've known her for about three years. I have business interests in San Jose. I've made a lot of money in Silicon Valley. I met Pam at a party at the home of the CEO of a company I am interested in. She was friendly, witty and comfortable in my company. To me she was something spectacular: a beautiful woman with superior intelligence. I am married, but you probably know that. However, my marriage has been less than satisfactory, and. . . ."

"You and Pam have had a little romance going, right?"

"Yes. But it was confined to San Jose and San Francisco. Pam never came here. Until just now, when she came to meet Cartwright. And I made it a point not to see her."

The man seemed genuinely troubled. His unshaven face was sallow and his thinning hair needed a good shampoo. He was one of those vain men who attempt to cover creeping baldness by carefully combing what's left over the top. It never works. The suit he was wearing probably cost $1,500, but that morning it looked like it was borrowed from somebody else.

I asked *the* question: "Did you kill Benjy Noble?"

His answer was an explosive, *"No!"*

"Do you have any idea who did?"

This time the answer did not come so quickly. "I've thought about it a great deal. The members of the cast? Well, certainly not Sally Morse."

"Thanks a lot, pal," I said.

"Sean Wetherby is a lightweight. Cordelia was like a mother to Benjy. At least, she appeared to be. Christy Burgess is an airhead. Templeton Hedges is a stuffed shirt. And that director, Maria Theresa O'Higgins, is spaced out much of the time. No, Riordan, I not only cannot imagine a motive among these people, I can't see any of them having the resolve to do the job."

"Ever hear of Gerald Stone?"

"A poor actor who tried out for the play. But he's gay and Benjy was attracted to him. He came to the house a couple of times. Benjy wouldn't stoop to using him in the play because he was a . . . friend. But he did . . . entertain him on several occasions. Then, a few nights before he was killed, Benjy came home and said that he had cut off Stone because he was 'boring'."

"Do you know if Stone might be the type to get angry enough to kill?"

"As I told you, I only saw the man two or three times. I have no idea of how he might behave under *any* set of circumstances."

"Go home and shave, Denby. I do not think you are in any particular danger. Somebody has singled you out as a logical suspect. Somebody who might be the murderer. Possibly because you resent having lost money on Benjy's early plays. Maybe because you could be suspected of being Benjy's secret lover. He was, after all, staying at your house. That somebody who wants to hang you for the murder is probably getting pretty edgy, and must be heavily into obfuscation."

Denby was shocked and indignant. The fear and nervousness fell away. "The few thousand dollars I blew on Benjy's early works amounted to nothing. I was certainly not sexually attracted to him. I may be something of a philanderer, Riordan, but not in that direction."

"So go home. Take a shower. Put on a clean shirt and go to your office. I don't know yet who it is that's trying to dump Benjy's murder in your lap, but I know whoever it is cannot be terribly shrewd. Go buy some more businesses."

Denby seemed to be somewhat relieved as he left my office. But that didn't help me at all. I was honest in telling him that I thought somebody was just blowing smoke at him with death threats and the symbol of the knife. But, goddamit, I still had no idea who the culprit was.

Just as Denby was clearing my office door, the phone rang.

"This is your wounded partner, Riordan-san. I'm home, Mama's in the kitchen, and I have followed your instructions."

"Reiko, how do you feel? Are you comfortable. Stay in bed, honey. What do you mean, instructions?"

"I caught Dr. Cartwright at the Beverly Hilton this morning just before he left for a meeting. I asked him what you asked me to ask him. He was a little irritated, but he thought about it."

"Well?"

"He remembered that in one session dealing with Benjy's early life, the knife was mentioned. Benjy had got it from his uncle for Christmas. He wasn't sure which Christmas. Benjy confessed that he had damaged some of the furniture with the knife, trying out all the gadgets. But there was something else, something more serious, that he refused to talk about. Cartwright thinks Benjy might have injured a person ... or an animal. Whatever happened, it was buried deep in his subconscious, and he didn't choose to let it out. Maybe he couldn't."

"Bless you, my child. Now rest and get well. Is there anything I can bring you?"

"Yeah, bring me a pizza. The hospital food was made out of cardboard and styrofoam, and Mama only knows Japanese food. I love Mama's food, you understand, and I am true to my heritage, but enough is enough. In a couple of days, a pepperoni pizza or a slab of barbecued ribs will taste mighty good. And pick up a good murder mystery. Something not too complicated. I don't like to play guessing games with those writers. Just get me something where the butler did it."

It did my old heart good to hear Reiko talking like her charming self once again. And her message set off a tiny fire in the back of my mind. Finally, I could see a small glimmering at the end of the tunnel.

39
"Then, one night he dumped me."

I WALKED OVER to the computer store on Calle Principal where Gerald Stone was employed. Stone was a late addition to the cast of this drama. I needed to size the man up myself. Nothing I had been told about him was very revealing. He had been Benjy's lover for a very short time. Benjy had dumped him because he was "boring," whatever that meant. Although I have met many men of the gay persuasion, some of whom have been my good friends, I was not convinced that a brief liaison like Stone's with Benjy could produce enough passion to inspire murder.

There was only one person visible when I walked in the store, a tall blond man wearing a white shirt with starched collar and a very conservative necktie. He was handsome to the point of being beautiful. His deep tan contrasted with his heavy blond mustache, and he walked toward me with an easy grace that made me feel a little uncomfortable.

"Yes, sir, what can we do for you this morning?"

"I'm looking for Gerald Stone."

"I'm Gerry Stone. Why me especially?"

"I understand that you were a friend of Benjy Noble. You must know that Benjy was murdered. I'm a private investigator hired by a person who shall be nameless to look into the circumstances surrounding his death. My name is Pat Riordan."

I studied the man's face for any reaction, but saw none. Stone looked sober and concerned. There was no hint of shock or nervousness.

"Yes, Mr. Riordan. I was a friend—or acquaintance would be the better word—of Benjy. I tried out for his new play early in July, when the first call went out. Unfortunately, I didn't get a part. But he and I became . . . rather close for a short time."

"Do you mind if I ask you when was the last time you saw Benjy?"

"Not at all. It was a couple of days before he died."

"At that time, did Benjy tell you he wanted to . . . break off the . . . friendship?"

I caught a small twitch that time. Stone looked away from me toward the store window. It was the first time his eyes had left mine.

I pursued the point: "Isn't it true that your relationship with Benjy was mainly . . . physical? That it was a homosexual relationship?"

He turned on me with fury in his eyes. "Who told you that? Denby, that horse's ass? That skinny little bastard Wetherby?"

"Look, Gerry, you don't have to answer my questions. I'm just a rent-a-cop. But I do have pretty good connections with the real police, and they listen to me. It might be easier for you to talk to me than have to sweat the Carmel cops."

He stood there a moment, studying the shine on his shoes. "We can't talk here, Riordan. Wait a minute."

Stone walked to the back of the store and spoke briefly to somebody I couldn't see. He came back to where I was standing and said, "Let's get out of here. There's a little place up the street where we can have privacy."

Neither of us said anything as we walked up Calle Principal to a small coffee shop. Stone led me to a booth in the back. There wasn't another soul in the place except a waitress. We both ordered coffee and stayed silent until we had been served. The waitress took up her position by the cash register near the front of the store.

Stone spoke first: "Nobody can hear us here. I'm going to tell you just what happened on the night that Benjy Noble was killed. If you try to hang me with it, I'll say you're lying and it'll be my word against yours."

"Go ahead, Gerry. It's your party."

"OK. I had been out with Benjy nearly every night for a couple of weeks. There was no question that everybody in the cast was aware of it. If they weren't, they just didn't dig the situation."

I thought of Sally, innocent, stage-struck Sally. Super-sophisticated Sally. *She* must have been unaware of the Stone connection.

"Then, one night he dumped me. I had picked him up as usual, but when he got in the car, he simply turned to me and said thanks a lot, but no thanks, know what I mean? I remember his words: 'You are beginning to bore me, Gerry.'"

"So then, did you punch him in the mouth?"

"Oh, no, I was just hurt. I had just got used to the fact that Benjy was up and down, happy and depressed, from hour to hour. But I had never expected him to spit in my face."

Stone put his head in his hands. Suddenly, he seemed not to be as young and beautiful as he had appeared in the store.

"I guess it all got out very quickly. Benjy told somebody in that way of his, swearing the person to secrecy. Then he told everybody else one at a time the same way. He was a duplicitous little bastard who told everybody his innermost feelings—in strictest confidence, of course.

"Anyway, the day after he dumped me, I got this strange phone call. I could hardly believe it at the time. But the caller wanted to enlist me in a plot. To get even, you know. What I was to do was to call Benjy and plead with him, you know.

He loved the bizarre and unusual, and more than anything else he loved the theater. If I invited him to meet me in the dead of night on the stage at the Forest Theater, he'd be intrigued by the idea of having sex at center stage. He'd come. But I was just simply to wait for him there and beat the bastard up. He deserved it for many sins, the caller said. I thought it was pretty crazy, but I was really pissed at the time, so I said sure, why not."

This was more than I had anticipated. Here was Gerald Stone, the failed actor, confessing to me that he had arranged to meet Benjy Noble on the stage at the Forest Theater with the full intent of beating him up.

"So, go on. You met him and you beat him to death. But why the knife in the throat?"

"Listen, Riordan, you've got to believe me. I met the guy and I worked him over. I left him lying in the middle of the stage. But he was alive. And I hadn't hurt him that bad. Cut up his face some, and left some lumps and bruises. But he was alive. Hey, he was even sitting up and calling me dirty names when I took off. The cops can get me for beating up on the guy, but not for murder. Never."

"Who was it that called you, Gerry. Must have been somebody you knew, or who knew you. Certainly, you wouldn't have responded so freely to an anonymous call."

"I was ready to do anything, Riordan. Benjy had romanced me and made me promises, then dropped me cold. I had a lot of hate at that time."

"You didn't answer my question."

He closed his eyes and cradled his coffee cup with both hands. "It was the old lady. Benjy's aunt. Cordelia Pompilio."

40
"There was little else I could do."

CORDELIA POMPILIO lived in a little house high on the
Carmel Hill. You'd never find San Pedro Lane unless you live
there or were taken by a native guide. I had a tough time finding the place myself, and I've been hanging around this pic-
turesque little village for thirty-five years. Some places you
just never go except in a case of life or death, or possibly a
dinner invitation, and this was one of them.

I parked outside a high grape-stake fence that hid the
house from the road, behind a rusty Pontiac that I figured
must be Cordelia's. The gate in the fence was ajar, so I walked
through. Two or three steps led down to the level on which
the house was built, and planter boxes filled with colorful
flowers lined the short path. I like colorful flowers but I can't
attach any names to them. These looked like what Sally called
"impatience." If that was the word. I always thought she was
kidding me.

The top of the Dutch door was open, so I called out:

"Cordelia. Mrs. Pompilio. Are you there?" It was dim inside
the house. While it had been sunny down in Monterey, the fog

was still swirling around up here on the hilltop. After a few moments I could see the back of Cordelia Pompilio's head over an armchair facing the enormous picture window that looked out on the higher elevations of Pebble Beach and the traffic on Highway One far below. She didn't appear to hear me.

I reached inside and opened the bottom half of the door. She didn't react to the sound. I was afraid she was asleep or maybe sick. Maybe even dead. I walked around her chair.

Cordelia was none of the above. Her eyes were wide open and she was contemplating the scenery that spread out beyond her picture window. Below her, the dense forest of the Del Monte Properties, with its hills and canyons. Just beyond, the ridge along which the Holman Highway runs, connecting Highway One to Pacific Grove. And beyond that, the Bay of Monterey, out of the fog, glistening bright blue in the sunlight.

"It's an inspiring sight, isn't it?" she said, with a beatific smile. "It's too bad Mr. Pompilio never got to see it. We were living in Salinas when he died. Salinas is nice, too, if you are in the lettuce business or love the rodeo. We were happy there. Until Benjy came to live with us."

I had to say *something*. "Cordelia, I'm Pat Riordan, remember? The private investigator. You came to see me at my office."

"I recognized you, Mr. Riordan. You needn't be so apologetic."

"I didn't mean to intrude, but I must talk with you. You see, I just had a conference with a man named Gerald Stone. He told me some things that were rather disturbing. You're the only person who can clarify them for me."

She closed her eyes and lay back in the chair. "It had to come to this sooner or later, didn't it? What is it that the poet said about the best laid plans of mice or men? They never work out, do they?"

"Cordelia, you had better tell me the whole story. Then maybe I'll be able to help you. I think whatever you did, you did out of an honest compulsion to right a wrong. Or several wrongs. Tell me."

Her voice was very low when she began to speak. "When Benjy came to live with us when my brother was still alive, he was already a very strange human being. He was bright. Oh, was he ever bright. He was nine—and he had read most of the classics. His vocabulary was incredible, and he wrote articles and stories that were printed in magazines that, I'm sure, had no idea of his age. It was his mother's influence, you know. Before she disappeared, she had spent nearly every hour with Benjy, reading to him, teaching him."

I interrupted: "What ever happened to Benjy's mother? I'm not too clear on that."

"She ran off. I told you that. Years later I heard that she died in an institution. Mental problems, you know. Benjy always blamed his father or Mr. Pompilio for her running away. He resented his father so much that he scarcely shed a tear when he died. And he hated Mr. Pompilio with a passion. Mr. Pompilio *tried* to make friends with the boy, but he would have none of it. He bought him things, nice things. But the only thing that Mr. Pompilio gave Benjy that he seemed to appreciate was a Swiss Army knife. You've seen the magazine article? With a picture of Benjy and his knife?"

"Was it the one Hal Denby got as a gift the other day?"

"Oh, yes. Denby, that awful man, was responsible for bringing Benjy back to Monterey. I hated him for it. It was a shameful thing for Benjy to come back to Monterey. When Mr. Pompilio sent him away to that military school, he never really came back here to live. He went directly to USC, and then to New York. But on one occasion, he did stay here a few days. Mr. Pompilio stayed out of the house when Benjy was here. He had a couch in his office in his Monterey restaurant and he would sleep there until Benjy had left. But one night . . . when he was in his office, the restaurant burned down, with Mr. Pompilio in it. Benjy had been out of the house that night, and when he returned he would not say where he had been. But I knew. The Monterey Fire Department discovered early the next morning that the fire had been deliberately set. There were no suspects. But I knew, and God is my witness, that Benjy set that fire. His uncle, my decent, loving husband had done everything he could for the boy. But he could not stomach Benjy's homosexuality. He made no secret of it. And Benjy killed him. He never admitted it to me, Mr. Riordan, but I *know.*"

"You said you resented Denby's bringing Benjy back to Monterey. Yet, you tried out for the play. And Benjy cast you in an important part. Does that make any sense?"

She sat up proudly. "He knew I had been a professional. He couldn't have made another choice. It's a good play. I would like to have played that part."

"Now, let me see if I've got this all straight. You were the person who made the threatening calls to Denby, right?"

"Yes. I wanted to frighten the man. There was little else I could do."

"And you knew about Benjy's relationship with Gerald Stone, and the fact that Benjy had dumped the guy. You didn't bother to conceal your identity when you called Stone."

"I saw no reason to. I simply told the man that I hated Benjy Noble as much as he did, and that I had an idea for revenge that might work well for both of us. Stone was very willing to cooperate."

"So they met at the theater in the middle of the night and Stone beat Benjy up. But he insists that Benjy was alive when he left him."

"Oh, yes, he was. But I was there, too, Mr. Riordan. I needed the satisfaction. I hoped that Stone might kill Benjy. But he left the job undone. When he went away, I seized a piece of firewood from the stack near one of the fireplaces, and I beat Benjy with it until he was really dead."

She showed no remorse or guilt. She spoke those last sentences proudly.

"That still doesn't explain the Swiss Army knife. What was that supposed to represent."

Cordelia stood up and walked to the great picture window and looked out over the serene, fog-shrouded hills.

"My husband gave Benjy such a knife—the one I sent to

Denby. He took it to a jeweler and had Benjy's name inlaid in silver. Benjy even thanked him. About that time, he had become interested in Satanism, and had read everything he could find about its rituals. Just before he went off to Caldwell Academy, he used that knife in one of his horrid rites. He sacrificed my cat, Mr. Riordan, and left her lying on the kitchen floor, with the long blade of the knife deep in her throat, and the other things all spread out in different directions. I bought a brand new knife and used it on Benjy. It was only justice, Mr. Riordan, only justice."

41
"Who'd he think he was, God?"

MUCH LATER, when I told Sally this story, all she could say was, "The sonofabitch killed a pussycat? How could any human being in the world do such a completely despicable thing?"

"Sal, you don't understand. Cordelia killed Benjy. She took the life of a human being."

"I don't care. The little shit deserved to die. Pulitzer Prize-winning playwright, my ass. He sure turned out to be a weird little beast. Who'd he think he was, God?" Which is what I have been saying about playwrights all along. They invent people. So, what the hell, they can kill 'em off if they feel like it.

The play went on as scheduled. The programs read Anna Leiser, but everybody knew it was a Benjy Noble play. Cordelia's part was offered to Alison Hargrove, but she turned it down, pleading poor health. I think the old girl had stage fright. I still don't know what she thought she heard on the night Benjy was killed. Maybe Cordelia's blows to the playwright's skull. Eventually, they found a woman in Pacific Grove who could play the role.

Reviews were mixed: "Benjy Noble's last play turned out to be a terrible mistake. Although the cast members did what they could with the lines, the play was just short of a disaster. The only redeeming feature was the performance of Christy Burgess, whose delicate beauty illuminated the Forest Theater stage." That was some guy on *The Herald* who had been sleeping with Christy for several weeks. Another: "I was mesmerized by the fascinating ritual on the stage at the Forest Theater last night. Benjy Noble's characters, all so terribly lost, sharing yet unknowing, stayed with me for hours after the play ended." That was a drama teacher from Monterey Peninsula College writing in one of the weekly throwaways. Still another: "Confusion reigned on the stage of the Forest Theater as Pulitzer Prize winner Benjy Noble's posthumously produced play was inflicted on an expectant audience last night. Standing out in the cast with an elegant, yet sensitive performance was Sally Morse as Katherine." I wrote that last one myself. It never got into print.

The whole mess about Benjy's murder and the long story behind it hit the papers several days before opening night. Which accounted for the capacity crowd that appeared on the coldest night of the summer. Audiences go for the macabre, even if it's secondhand. Some were more interested in inspecting the stage for bloodstains than in seeing the famous playwright's last produced work. About thirty people left at intermission. But I stayed on the the bitter end, with Reiko beside me, wrapped in a blanket, muttering bitterly. Her mama-san sat on the other side of her with no expression on her face. She has lived in this country all her life and still prefers not to speak English. It was Reiko's first night out, and it was a mistake. "You could have taken me to see *Batman Returns*," she said.

She was able to muster a pleasant expression after the play and offer her congratulations to Sally. "You were great," she said. I kissed Sally and said, "She's right, you know. You *were* great. How long is the run?"

"Four days. Tonight, Friday, Saturday, and Sunday.

They're cutting it short because of the, you know, circumstances. It's really been a topic of conversation in Carmel. Cordelia has a lot of friends in this town."

"OK. I'll see you Sunday night after the show. We'll go out and celebrate."

"Not until Sunday night? What's the matter with you, Riordan? Can't stand culture?"

"I want you to get your rest, honey. The theater is a stern taskmaster. Or so I've heard. Goodnight. I've got to take the Masudas home."

Sally grabbed me and planted a long, damp kiss on me, and I felt her hand on my behind. "There," she said, "that'll hold you for a couple of days."

Reiko and Mama-san were more than pleased to see me break free. I drove them to Reiko's flat, helped her up the stairs under Mama-san's disapproving gaze, and returned to my Carmel cottage.

Gerry Stone, whose real name was Leroy Weaver, gave himself up to the Carmel police and was charged with assault with intent to do bodily harm. Cordelia told her long, complicated story to Lieutenant Miller, and was jailed until her lawyer got her out on her own recognizance. "Couldn't do anything else, Pat," Miller told me. "She admitted killing the guy, so she had to go to jail. I think she's got a good insanity plea, though. And her lawyer seems like a pretty competent guy."

I have a confession to make, though. *Waiting for the L-Train* was not destined to become my all-time favorite play, but I went back to see it three more times. Sally was dead wrong. That kiss *didn't* hold me for a couple of days.

Or nights.

ABOUT THE AUTHOR

Roy Gilligan was born during the first half of the twentieth century on the south bank of the Ohio River near where the great stream admits the Licking. He was nearly famous for a very short while in Cincinnati as a TV-radio personality. In the late fifties and early sixties he wrote a weekly column on advertising for the *San Francisco Chronicle*. Later on he contributed book reviews to that same newspaper and articles to the *San Jose Mercury-News*, the *Monterey Herald*, and *San Francisco Focus* magazine, among many others. For two decades he taught English in California high school. He lives with his first and only wife in Carmel, California. He has a daughter, Robin, who supervised the cover design of this book, two remarkable grandchildren, and sweet memories of four wonderful dogs: Wendy, Tina, Maggie, and Mandy Lou.

This is the fifth book in the Pat Riordan Mystery series. If you enjoyed it, and want to pursue any of the first four—*Chinese Restaurants Never Serve Breakfast, Live Oaks Also Die, Poets Never Kill,* and *Happiness is Often Deadly*—please send $8.95 plus $1.50 postage and handling to

Brendan Books
Post Office Box 221143
Carmel, California 93922-1143

(California residents add appropriate sales tax.)

These books are available through bookstores that use the R.R. Bowker Company *Books In Print* catalog system, and are distributed to the trade through Capra Press.

Death Under an Orange Tree

(The author of this book, a whimsical chap with an uneven temper, is hard at work on his next in the series. It may or may not appear under the above title.)

Chapter One

When I knocked on Armand's door that morning, I really didn't know what to expect. He had called me the night before, in a sort of panic, summoning me to his house in hushed and mysterious tones to discuss something of "vital importance."

Now, I knew that over the years the only thing of really "vital importance" to Armand was the bottom line. How much the restaurant made, how many bottles of wine were sold, how much profit. So I wasn't too excited. The guy has caught one of his trusted employees stealing, I thought after his call. I hope it wasn't one of his relatives. He wants me to bus dishes for him so that I can sneak up on the culprit. But all of his people know me. That couldn't be it.

I didn't hear any sound in the house after my first knock, so I knocked again, pretty hard. Still nothing. I waited about thirty seconds and then pounded the door with my fist, yelling "Armand, dammit, I know you're in there."

Soft sounds, like bare feet on plush carpet, came from within. The door opened slightly. Armand's large brown eyes looked at me through a six-inch space. I tried to push through, but he held the door tightly against me.

"I'm sorry, Pat. I heard you the first time. I was awake. The trouble is--well, it really isn't trouble--I can't find my pants. I know I took them off last night. But this morning I can't find them. You know how it is."

"I do not know how it is, Armand. There have been times when I have misplaced my wallet or lost my keys. But I have always found my pants. Where the hell did you leave them?"

The door opened a little wider and I was able to slip through. He was standing before me, clean-shaven and impeccably groomed, but with no pants. I was surprised to note that his legs, which I had never seen before, were rather thin and knobby, and his toenails were badly in need of a trim. But he was wearing boxers and he looked for all the world like a bewildered Carmel summer tourist who had just discovered that the ocean breezes can really affect a man's virility when they sneak up his floppy shorts.

"Come in, come in," he said. He did not look at me directly, searching the room, it seemed, for the missing pants.

I tried to sympathize. "Armand, you must have other pants. Why don't you just put a pair on and let it go at that? The lost ones will show up."

"It isn't that," he said. "Jennifer was here last evening, and--well, things got a bit passionate. I flung caution to the winds . . . and I must have flung my pants with it. It's just not like me."

True. Armand is usually completely in charge. Nothing escapes his eagle eye in the restaurant. He personally supervises the filling of each bottle at the winery. But that morning he was completely unstrung because he couldn't find his pants.

"Sit down, Pat, please." He collapsed onto a sofa, half sitting, half reclining. I took a chair across the room.

He had regained his composure to a degree. He finally looked directly at me. "Pat, you have known me quite a long while. You know that I am not easily disturbed. And you know how close-knit my family is." He hid his face in his hands for a long moment and let me sit there twiddling my thumbs.

"So, go ahead, Armand. What's buggin' you? Woman trouble? Embezzlement? Hemorrhoids? What?"

He sat up straight on the couch. "You know of my treasured aunt in Miami?"

"No, Armand. I have never heard of an aunt in Florida. I thought your whole damn' family was here." I was getting a little irritated.

"She is my favorite, Pat. She has been living there alone for many years. But I have not heard from her in several months. And during the past week, I have called her frequently, but her phone does not answer. I am afraid of foul play."

"Doesn't she have any friends? Can't you get in touch with somebody who knows about her?"

"She has been something of a recluse. I do not know the names of any of her acquaintances. I am stumped, Riordan."

"So what do you want me to do? Call the Miami cops? Enter a missing persons report? Goddamit, Armand, what can I do from here?"

He took a deep breath. "I want you to go to Miami and find my aunt. Or at least discover what has happened to her. I, of course, will pay all your expenses, plus a reasonable fee."

That shook me up a bit. "Reasonable fee" shook me up. Armand was very cagey with a buck. But what really shocked me was his request that I go to Miami.

"Armand, I don't go to Miami. I seldom leave California. I'm licensed as a private investigator only in California. Now, maybe if I got in touch with Travis McGee, but he's not really a PI...."

"Don't jest with me, Pat. This is a serious matter. And you're the only investigator I know." He rose from the couch and walked to a desk in the corner of the room. From a drawer, he extracted a huge check book, one of those deals with three or four checks to a page.

"How much do you require as an advance? Two thousand? Three thousand? Five thousand?"

"Armand, I'm trying to tell you that I just don't go to Florida. I have no authority there. I have little enough here. Reiko couldn't handle things without me." I knew that last was an out-and-out lie. Reiko could very well handle things without me. Maybe she might even prefer to do without me for a while.

"Take her with you. You see, Riordan, my aunt is very important to me. I will spare no expense."

There wasn't very much I could do. Business hadn't been all that overwhelming on the Monterey Peninsula. We were in a fairly dry period. Maybe, just maybe, it wouldn't be so bad. Maybe it'd be fun.

"I'll have to ask Reiko, Armand. She's my partner, you know. She's got to approve or

disapprove. But I'll ask. When do you need to
know?"

"Yesterday, Riordan. Here's your check. Five
thousand dollars. Of course, I want every bit
accounted for."

"You hold it for now, Armand. I--I really
don't know if this thing will fly."

"It will fly." He tucked the check into my
shirt pocket. "I want you on your way
tomorrow."

Armand can be a very forceful guy, even
without his pants. When he made up his mind
about something, it was like cast in bronze.

I left the house a little dazed. It was
perfectly true that I hadn't been away from the
West Coast for quite a stretch. Some of my
California cases had led me to connections in
Washington, Oregon, and Nevada. But I had not
been east of Reno for I don't know how many
years.

Driving from Armand's house on Casanova in
Carmel to my office on Alvarado Street in
Monterey, I began to feel better about the
mission upon which I was probably about to
embark. But what about Reiko? And what about
Sally? Sally is the lady of my choice, a Carmel
travel agent who warms my heart and my bed, but
will not marry me. How will she feel about my
flying off to the East?

I shook off all my doubts as I hit the top
of Carmel Hill and took the Munras off-ramp
into Monterey. But at that time, I really
didn't know what was in store for me. That trip
to Miami brought me more grief than I ever
anticipated. If I had known--even suspected--I
would have told Armand to stick his five
thousand bucks up where the sun don't shine.